Love
in the Rain

Naguib Mahfouz

Translated by
Nancy Roberts

The American University in Cairo Press
Cairo   New York

First published in 2011 by
The American University in Cairo Press
113 Sharia Kasr el Aini, Cairo, Egypt
420 Fifth Avenue, New York, NY 10018
www.aucpress.com

Dar el Kutub No. 15028/10
ISBN 978 977 416 452 1

Dar el Kutub Cataloging-in-Publication Data

Mahfouz, Naguib, 1911–2006
        Love in the Rain/ Naguib Mahfouz; translated by Nancy Roberts.
    —Cairo: The American University in Cairo Press, 2010
        p.   cm.
        ISBN 978 977 416 452 1
    1. Arabic fiction   2. Title   I. Roberts, Nancy (tr.)
        892.73

1 2 3 4 5 6 7 8   15 14 13 12 11

Designed by Andrea El-Akshar
Printed in Egypt

1

Surrounded by an uninterrupted stream of people colliding with one another from all directions and a medley of sounds coming from high and low—a raucous collage of all the colors of the rainbow—the two of them walked along side by side without saying a word. She was clad in a short brown dress, her black hair flowing loosely about her head and down over her brow. As for him, he sported a blue shirt and gray trousers, his hair combed neatly to the right. Her eyes were honey-colored and inquisitive, and his, slightly protruding, which perfectly complemented his straight, pointed nose. As she gave herself over to the walk, he bided his time, waiting for an opportunity.

"The crowd's unbearable," he said.

"But it's amusing," she murmured with a smile.

He took her reply as a charming maneuver, nothing more. In fact, it seemed like a response to the desire of his heart. Gesturing with his muscular arm in the direction of the Haroun al-Rashid Café, he found her turning to go there with him without hesitation. They made their way to the garden behind the restaurant, where they chose a semi-secluded seat under a trellis of English ivy. They looked around at the place, then at each other. Though he voiced no complaint, he felt somewhat oppressed by the muggy heat.

As he ordered two glasses of lemonade, he was dying to talk about what was on his mind. However, he said to himself: Let the words come on their own, and in their own time. Surely that's better.

"The days we spent at the university seem like a dream now . . . ," he said.

Completing his sentence, she added, ". . . with its joys and sorrows."

"It'll only be a few months now before we both start our jobs."

She nodded in agreement, then wondered aloud, "But where's the world headed?"

This was the question that confronted him, always and everywhere. Where indeed? Would it be war, or peace? And the flood of rumors?

"Let it head wherever it wants to."

They drank lemonade until they had tears in their eyes.

"How's your brother Ibrahim?" he asked.

"He's fine. He doesn't write much, but he comes home from the front once a month."

Then, as though she wanted to make excuses for him, she said, "Marzouq, if you weren't an only child, you would have been drafted just like him."

He made no comment, and together they gave themselves over to the silence. Feeling another urge to talk about what was on his mind, he said with a laugh, "We shouldn't try to make our tryst look so innocent!"

"So, then," she replied with a playful look in her eyes, "our tryst *is* an innocent one!"

Reverting to a serious tone, he said, "I mean the subject my sister Saniya spoke to you about."

"You've had your share of girlfriends, to my knowledge," she replied warily.

Even more serious now, he continued, "We often act out of a need for diversion. But there comes a time when nothing will satisfy us but true love."

2

"True love?"

"That's exactly what I mean, Aliyat."

After some hesitation, she asked, "Don't you think it's too early for you to get married?"

"That's what the older generation says," he replied contemptuously. "But time's of no importance as long as we're in control of our fates."

Sounding concerned, she asked, "Are you sure of your feelings?"

He gazed at her affectionately and said, "One of my main faults is that I'm not good at expressing my feelings. How many times have we met? Even so, I've never once complimented you on your beauty or your sophistication."

She made no reply.

"Why don't you say anything?" he asked fervently.

"I don't know," she said with a sigh. "I guess I'm afraid."

"The truth is," he said tenderly, "I love you more than anything in the world."

"That's better," she murmured with a smile.

He laughed happily.

"And I've got something even nicer to tell you."

"The fact is," she admitted, "I haven't been a passive observer of the battle, and you know that."

Elated now, he said, "Consider me mad about you!"

Lowering her eyes, she whispered, "And I'm happy, since I feel the same way about you."

Flooded with joy and inspiration, he said, "I would rather have experienced this happiness in a place where we could be alone, just the two of us."

The two of them laughed together, then fell silent as their eyes met. He suggested that they go to a park.

As they got up to leave, she said, "Don't forget that there will be troubles along the way!"

2

It was midnight, and the Inshirah coffeeshop on Sheikh Qamar Street had no more customers. The only employees still around were the waiter, Amm Abduh Badran, and Ashmawi the shoe shiner. Ponderous and lethargic, Ashmawi ambled outside and squatted next to the coffeeshop entrance, where he sat on his heels staring, bleary-eyed, at nothing in particular. As for Amm Abduh, he sat down on a chair in the middle of the entrance and lit a cigarette. Fifteen minutes later a white Mercedes passed the coffeeshop, then stopped at a nearby curb.

Ashmawi looked up and said, "It's Husni Higgawi."

Amm Abduh rose to receive the newcomer. Clad in a white suit and the picture of elegance, he sauntered toward them with his tall, lean physique and his massive head. He greeted both men by name, then took his seat. Meanwhile, Amm Abduh went to get the shisha and Ashmawi scooted up next to him to shine his shoes. Since Husni Higgawi was the only customer who came after midnight—whenever he had the time—he and the two elderly men had exchanged many a conversation, and an intimate bond of sorts had developed between them.

Amm Abduh was sixty years old, and if the truth be told, Husni Higgawi was taken by the man's dignified bearing, his aging waiter's uniform, the reddish round bald spot on his head, and the heavy but kind look in his eyes. He'd also taken a liking to Ashmawi, whose age no one knew, but which he estimated at somewhere between seventy and eighty. He was moved by the sight of Ashmawi's huge, languid figure as though it were a living relic from his days as the neighborhood thug. He had great respect for the man's endurance on life's battlefield despite failing health, diminished hearing and sight, and the loss of the glory he'd once known.

Amm Abduh devoted special care to Husni Higgawi's shisha, not only on account of the tip he would get in return, but also because he knew it was the secret behind his visits to the Inshirah coffeeshop. Another reason Husni Higgawi frequented the place was his nostalgia for Sheikh Qamar Street, the place where he'd been born. He was fifty years old, yet he exuded a remarkable vitality and had yet to sprout a single gray hair. He seemed genuinely to enjoy his time at the humble coffeeshop with his two comrades and his long tête-à-têtes with the shisha. The conversation started off as usual with the fighting on the front, questions about the near and distant future, and tactfully worded inquiries about the well-being of Amm Abduh's son Ibrahim and other young men from Darb al-Hilla, Ashmawi's hometown, who'd been drafted into the war. Husni Higgawi saw Ashmawi as typical of the masses with whom he would otherwise have no dealings and who were sincerely keen to fight—unconditionally, fearlessly, and without a thought for the consequences. He thought to himself: After all, what do they have to fear, when all they have to their names is dignity and a fairy tale? Then he thought: The people who are really suffering are the true patriots.

When Ashmawi had finished shining Husni Higgawi's shoes, Amm Abduh came up to where he was sitting and, leaning toward him slightly, said, "My daughter Aliyat has been proposed to by a young man who studied with her."

"Congratulations, Amm Abduh!" he replied with genuine interest.

In a tone that was pleased but subdued, Amm Abduh replied, "It's good for a girl to get married. But like her, the groom doesn't have a job yet."

"That's the way things go these days."

"I'm strapped with heavy financial burdens, and as you know, the only one of my sons who's finished his education has been drafted."

Husni Higgawi rejoined with confidence, "Your daughter is educated, and she's aware of all these things. So, what do they say about the groom?"

"He's broke!" the man replied bitterly. "His father's in the same boat as I am, a clerk at some commercial establishment."

"Has his son been drafted?"

"He's exempt because he's their only son. The rest of his children are girls. One of them is a classmate and close friend of Aliyat's." Husni Higgawi savored a long puff on the shisha and thought to himself: The good-hearted waiter is also living a fairy tale. The truth could crush him. Our morals are an illusion. They're based on nothing but profit.

Then he said to Amm Abduh, "There are some shrewd girls who prefer to marry a well-to-do middle-aged man as a way of finding stability in life."

"I don't know," the man said, shaking his head in bewilderment.

"In any case, your daughter isn't one of them."

"God be with her!"

"Amen!" Husni Higgawi replied, concealing a sardonic smile.

Then, with sudden enthusiasm, Amm Abduh said, "Aliyat is an ambitious girl. She worked to bring in an income even when she was a student. She made so much money from translation, she was able to dress in a way that suits university life even though I couldn't provide any of that for her."

"She's a real go-getter."

"But has she saved enough to be able to furnish even a single room?"

"That's the question."

"For her, that type of thing doesn't even matter."

"It's a generation that deserves to be commended!" Husni Higgawi replied with a chuckle. His thoughts wandered to his elegant apartment on Sherif Street and he said to himself: The real struggle in this life is between facts and fairy tales.

"Haven't you ever thought of getting married, sir?" queried Amm Abduh.

"Never." Then, pointing at him warningly with his forefinger, he added, "And I've never regretted it!"

He recalled how, during a brief news report at the studio, a journalist had asked him and a number of other people working on the film about their philosophy of life. He also remembered how, when he'd been asked the question, he'd gone pale and not been able to come up with an answer.

So then, did he really not have a philosophy of life?

3

Precious indeed were the few hours Ibrahim Abduh got to spend in Cairo. His sister Aliyat placed her arm in his and they made their way through a great press of people beneath a flood of lights. Clad in his military uniform, he bore a palpable resemblance to his sister, especially his honey-colored eyes, despite his slightly pug nose, thick lips, and husky build. He was devouring everything with his senses and being bombarded by one feeling after another. Sometimes for a fleeting moment he would enter a bizarre realm of existence somewhere between reality and fantasy, or vacillate between reality and fantasy in his thoughts.

His sister asked him, "How are you handling the transition tonight from being rocked by explosions somewhere underground to the world of noisy, drunken Cairo? Is it a shock?"

She recalled to the letter words he had spoken at an earlier time in response to the same question.

However, he replied casually, "It's become a routine."

"And your usual resentment?"

"It's become a routine, too," he said in the same tone.

Then he added with a smile, "Death itself has become a daily routine."

Stepping aside to avoid a young man rushing past like a torpedo, she asked him gently, "How do you want us to live?"

"I don't want to change the order of the universe. All I want is to feel that I'm being received by my friends as someone who's coming back from a blazing war front in defense of the homeland."

She made no reply, so he went on, "I'm not asking for a twenty-one-gun salute. All I want is a bit of concern and seriousness."

"But the war is all people talk about!"

"That's not enough . . . ."

Then, after some hesitation, he added, "But I guess it's understandable."

"Damn it!" she shot back, "whatever is or has been, death is real."

Then, squeezing his arm, she said, "Don't let anything ruin an hour of happiness for you. Let's have some sandwiches, then go see a movie."

He made no objection. However, he added, "It's strange that I'd never met your fiancé Marzouq before."

"Don't you like him?"

"He seems nice, but his sister seems nicer!"

She looked at him attentively as they stood in the shade near a corner coffee stand.

"Saniya?" she asked.

"Yeah. She's your friend, isn't she?"

"A good friend. She graduated a year before I did, and she works at the Agricultural Reform Office now. So you like her?"

"Quite a lot," he said.

"Love at first look?" Aliyat asked with a giggle.

"I think I must have won about a hundred looks from her," he said with a laugh.

"And all that behind our backs?"

"What matters . . . "

When he said nothing more, she asked, "What matters . . . ?"

" . . . is whether she'd be suitable as a wife."

"What are the conditions for suitability, in your view?"

"As you know, we're a conservative family."

"I can see that you've adopted Dad's ways of thinking."

"What matters to me is morals."

She drew his attention to a racy film advertisement that was nearly raw sex, and warned, "Lower your voice."

"You're conservative yourself, at least where morals are concerned."

"I appreciate your high opinion of me."

"And now, tell me . . . ."

"Based on what I know of her," she said with some exasperation, "she's a wonderful girl."

"I don't want to worry."

Laughing sympathetically, she said, "No soldier should be worried about what's going on in the city!"

Suddenly the lights went out, and the street went pitch black. Youthful cheers went up in a spirit of buffoonery amid the piercing cries of warning sirens on cars. Ibrahim tensed and his head was flooded with the echoes of rapid orders to get ready and hunker down into position. But then he heard Aliyat's gentle voice saying, "The lights go off a lot for unknown reasons."

Regaining his composure, he grasped her hand and stepped backward with her until their backs were up against the wall of the coffee stand.

"Does it last long?" he asked.

"Anywhere from a minute to an hour," she replied. "Just depends on our luck!"

It wasn't long before his eyes had adjusted to the darkness.

"What do you advise?" he asked her.

"Let's wait until the lights come back on."

"I mean, about Saniya!"

Laughing, she said, "Oh, Saniya! If you love her, marry her."

"Love isn't the problem!"

"So," she queried sarcastically, "what judgment would we make about you if we took your past into account?"

"Men aren't the same as women!" She stamped her foot angrily but didn't say a word.

Then he went on, "So, you don't want to tell me what you think."

"I said she was a great girl and that you should marry her if you love her," she snapped.

"I'll be seeing her tomorrow morning."

"So then," Aliyat asked with giggle, "why do they turn out the lights when the most masterly conspiracies are hatched in broad daylight?"

4

The temperature wasn't very high, but the rays of the sun poured down in blistering torrents. Beneath the streams of sunlight, the Fish Park, vacant or nearly so, extended far into the distance. The first to arrive, the two of them strolled about aimlessly as Ibrahim thought to himself: Just like Adam and Eve. Like Adam and Eve before they sinned. He grinned at the thought in spite of himself. Picking up on his facial expression, Saniya asked shyly, "Why are you smiling?"

Flustered, Ibrahim replied, "Because I'm happy!"

He opened his palms to the rays of the sun and said, "There's a place to sit in the grotto."

They headed toward the grotto, their nostrils filled with the fragrance of grasses moistened by the spray of water.

Well-proportioned, with limpid green eyes, she was of medium height or slightly less, the top of her chestnut head just barely coming up to his shoulder. They sat down side by side on a bench made from a palm tree stump.

"It's a blessing that you've come," he said.

"We aren't strangers," she replied modestly. "We're all one family."

The underground vault was dimly lit, and as often happens in places that are never visited by the sun, a sultry breeze blew.

Their eyes had communicated so much the day before that they didn't feel like total strangers. He noticed her looking curiously at his uniform.

"Do you have any family members who've been drafted?" he asked.

She shook her head, and he continued, "But even being drafted doesn't prevent people from thinking about the future as though they were going to live forever!"

"The length of our lives is in God's hands alone," she replied with sweet fervor.

He smiled with assent and relief, thinking to himself: I can't bring up the subject without any preliminaries. At the same time, it won't do for the preliminaries to go on too long, since we won't have another chance to see each other for another whole month—that is, if there's going to be another chance.

She may have been having similar thoughts. However, she managed to find a way out.

"Life there must be really hard," she said.

He felt grateful for her comment, the likes of which he wasn't accustomed to hearing from anyone but his family.

"Harder than you can imagine!"

"How do you bear it?"

He replied candidly, "I've come to believe that a person can live in hell itself and eventually get used to it."

Then, looking over at her attentively, he said, "But that doesn't prevent a person from looking for happiness and contentment."

She smiled bashfully, her wheat-colored cheeks suddenly pink. She seemed pleased.

He thought to himself: She's neither a child nor an actress. On the contrary, she's got a strong character and morals.

"Do you think the war will start up again?" she asked.

As though he hadn't heard her question, he said, "It seems you're not engaged?"

"So then, you've been asking around about me!"

"We have a mutual friend: Aliyat."

"And why are you worrying about things that don't concern you?"

"She congratulated me on my interest in you."

"Really?"

Then, in a suggestive tone he said, "And she wished me happiness and success."

They fell silent for a while, filled with contentment. He felt certain that he'd passed an important milestone, and that not a moment of his precious time had been spent in vain.

As for her, she decided to evade his glances.

"Why didn't you answer my question about whether the war will start up again?" she asked.

Intoxicated with emotion, he said, "I've talked about things that are certain, such as my admiration for you."

"But you don't know anything about me."

"The heart knows more than the mind can imagine!"

She murmured something in a voice too low for him to hear.

"What are you saying?" he asked. "You haven't said anything yet."

Then simply, candidly, and without hesitation she announced, "I'm happy!"

A look of gratitude glinted in his eyes as he enveloped one of her hands affectionately in both of his.

"Next time we'll take a decisive step," he said. "Until then, I'll be living a life that's rich and new in spite of everything."

"May God protect you from all harm."

"I've won a new heart that will feel with me somehow," he said blissfully.

She pondered his words.

Picking up on her thoughts, he said, "It seems that no one feels with me but my family."

His words flustered her momentarily. Then, as if to apologize on others' behalf she said, "This is a new experience for us. That's the reality of it. But what about what ought to be? Mr. Husni thinks it's a preplanned policy."

"Who's Mr. Husni?"

"He's a senior employee in our department at the government agency where I work."

"What does he mean?"

"What he means is that they don't want to mobilize the people for war until it's time to enter the battle."

"I don't understand!"

"Neither do I. Nobody claims to understand. Will the war start up again?"

"Those of us on the front think it will."

"As for those of us here, we can hardly believe it!"

"How do you all assess things?"

"You hear every imaginable contradiction."

With a chuckle Ibrahim said, "What you all want is to find victory announced in the morning newspaper one of these days!"

She laughed, and through laughter the two of them were released from the shackles of their anxiety. So, having returned to the topic at hand in the grotto, they exchanged a long, tender look of apology.

5

Husni Higgawi got up from where he'd been seated on the couch. His towering figure projected itself across the sitting room like a giant's shadow. Here in his apartment he experienced total comfort and a sense of being in full control. The sofas and chairs were as good for reclining as they were for sitting, and gadgets designed to provide ease and entertainment were situated in the corners alongside a variety of ornamental flourishes, including *objets d'art* arranged neatly along shelves displaying Japanese art and wares from Khan al-Khalili. Somewhere deep inside, he felt that these things cemented his relationship to the world and warded off the threat of annihilation. He moved over to the bar, where he filled two glasses with a cocktail he'd mixed himself with patience and expertise. Then he came back to the center of the room and placed one glass on the arm of an easy chair, an inch away from Saniya's hand.

Stirring his glass while still standing, he said, "To your health."

He emptied his glass, then added, "This room has witnessed farewells to many a loved one."

"You're a generous man in life and love," Saniya told him.

Changing the subject, he said, "Luckily, I've finally gotten an excellent film that's a whole fifteen minutes long."

Saniya smiled tepidly, recalling the way she'd screamed when she saw her first film. It had been years ago, and she'd been a student either in university or high school. The surprise had been overwhelming, and horrifying.

"Aliyat's finished," he said regretfully. "It's a terrible loss."

"She's engaged and getting ready for married life. What do you expect?"

"Well," he teased, "there's nothing wrong with letting one-self play up till the wedding!"

Fixing her green eyes on him, she said tellingly, "The thought of marriage suffocates a woman all over again."

"But many a married woman . . . !"

"That's another matter," Saniya interrupted. Then, with a laugh, she added, "Don't you want love to be respected even for a day or so?"

"I tried to talk her out of it."

"Is she really that important to you?"

"Years spent together are always precious to me."

Laughing derisively this time, she said, "It often occurs to me that all the women who walk down Sherif Street are either on their way to your apartment, or on their way back from it . . . ."

Husni Higgawi guffawed.

"Any woman who pokes fun at this apartment is an ingrate!"

"And as you can see, I've come to bid it farewell with all due respect."

"Even you, Saniya?" he exclaimed with a grin.

Pleased, she said, "It's my turn now, Your Highness."

"His father told me about him. He's a soldier, is he not?"

"That's right."

"Happiness is written all over your face."

"He's a kind, nice-looking young man."

"So just like that, you've decided to abandon the nest like your friend, Aliyat?"

"I'll love whoever wants to marry me!"

He thought to himself: Woman is the epitome of wisdom, and she's the only creature on earth that deserves to be adored.

However, to her he said mischievously, "So, it's a marriage of convenience."

"I really do love him," she replied hurriedly, a tone of concern evident in her voice. "Believe me."

"I believe you," he said. "But I'll be ever so sorry to see you go."

"You'll never be lonely in this apartment."

"But it's a way station, nothing more."

"The same thing could be said about any other place as well."

He retreated to the couch and sat down. He closed his eyes for a while, then said, "I visited the front recently as part of a delegation of cinematic photographers, and I took pictures of a half-abandoned Port Said. Have you ever seen a ghost town?"

"No, I haven't."

"It's like a nightmare!"

"I visited Port Said for a day once before the war."

"I lived there for three weeks while we were filming *Girl from Palestine* several years ago. It's a city that goes to sleep like any other city. But it can wake up at any hour of the night when a ship comes in, and before you know it, it's pulsating with life. There would be movement everywhere, lights blazing, the temperature rising. And in the evenings, you would hear the most captivating folk songs wafting on the air from the direction of the port."

"And you found it deserted?"

"Unlike other cities, it wasn't affected."

She fell silent for a while, then asked, "Do you suppose the war will start up again?"

"Conditions won't be right for it any time soon," he said with a shake of the head. "And no one would encourage us to let it happen. However, patient endurance on our part will provide us with the ideal conditions after the June defeat."

"The soldiers want war."

"That's only natural. And so does the public. As for us, we don't know what we want." Then, with a sigh he said, "Oh, my dear homeland!"

"As for us," she added bitterly, "we've stopped believing in anything."

"You're the children of the revolution, and you've got to solve your problems with us."

Changing his tone of voice, he asked, "Another glass?"

She declined with a shake of the head.

"I said I got an excellent film!"

"Do you remember *The Priest and the Bread Vendor*?"

"That's the one about a man and two women, then another strange man snatches them up!"

Suddenly she asked, "Why don't you get married before you miss your chance?"

"I've already missed my chance, dear."

"There's always a suitable wife to be found somewhere."

"Find something nice to say, or don't say anything at all . . . ."

"Do you respect your life?" she asked daringly.

"I've never thought about evaluating it."

"What pains me," she said, "is that I surrendered because I wanted to be able to buy things. They were necessary things, but still . . . ."

"Society is based on give and take," he said sympathetically. "So don't let it cause you pain."

Stamping the ground with her dainty foot, she demanded, "So when will we see the new film?"

6

Apart from the intermittent gurgling of the shisha, the Inshirah coffeeshop was awash in silence. Ashmawi was having his supper—a round of pita bread and some ta'miya—at the door, while Abduh Badran sat a short distance away from

Husni Higgawi, ready to make conversation or be of service. Husni Higgawi wondered to himself: How does a man like Abduh Badran, the head of a huge household, cope with the obscene cost of living? How can he possibly balance his limited budget even if all they eat is bread, all they have to wear are odds and ends from second-hand stores, and they all live together in one room? Yet, in spite of it all, his children have all gone to school, and two of them—Ibrahim and Aliyat— have finished university. So what miracles are being performed behind believers' backs?

He said to himself: What I spend in one night would support an entire family for several months. Yet I'm never without something to grumble about, and if a couple of months go by without work on a film, be it long or short, I start to fret. So what's the secret behind Amm Abduh's dignified, serene countenance? Aliyat told him she'd kept up with the fashions expected of a young co-ed with the cash she earned from translation, and the good-hearted man believed her. Never once did it occur to him that it was *my* money that was helping to support his daughter's university education. The day I found out that Aliyat was Amm Abduh's daughter, I got a bit nervous and felt some pangs of conscience. However, I put my misgivings to death with my cold mind. I said to myself: I don't believe in any of that, and my respect for Aliyat has never been shaken. On the contrary, I said: Damn them! They stand by and watch people be hurt, oppressed, and enslaved, but when they're faced with love and enjoyment, they turn into rapacious lions.

He was about to ask Amm Abduh how he coped with life's demands. However, he quickly abandoned the idea for fear of spoiling their peaceful midnight session, or of encouraging him with his question to ask for a loan or some other type of help.

Seeing that Husni Higgawi hadn't said anything for a while, Amm Abduh spoke up.

"Ibrahim's gotten engaged to Saniya, Marzouq's sister."

Having heard the news himself earlier, he'd given the bride a gift of money just as he had Aliyat before her. However, he replied, "May God preserve the bride and bring the groom happiness!"

"They're good folks and, like us, they just barely make ends meet. She works in the Agricultural Reform Department."

Ashmawi's voice came from the direction of the door, saying, "I don't like women who work!"

"All the girls in Darb al-Hilla are going to school, and the older ones are employees," rejoined Amm Abduh.

"Is that so!" exclaimed the old man scornfully.

"If you had a daughter, you'd think differently."

"I've got four children, all of them sons," he announced proudly.

This was the first time Husni Higgawi had heard about Ashmawi's sons.

"What do your sons do, Ashmawi?" he queried.

"Two of them are between fifty and sixty years old, and they work at the slaughterhouse."

Then he added limply, "The third was run over by the tram, and the fourth is in prison."

They all fell silent for a minute as they pondered the unsettling news. Then Husni Higgawi asked Amm Abduh, "Will Ibrahim get married right away, or will he postpone it until peace time?"

"That's his business, though I'd prefer that he get married sooner rather than later. But when will the war be over?"

"Who knows, Amm Abduh?"

"Really, who knows? And they're suffering like heroes."

"You're right."

"Even so, no one's concerned about them."

"That's not true. It's just that people still haven't gotten over the bitterness of the defeat."

Talk of the war drew Ashmawi inside the coffeeshop. Approaching with his huge frame, he said, "But God will give us the victory in the end."

"Say, 'God willing,'" interjected Husni Higgawi.

"Nothing happens apart from His will anyway," rejoined Ashmawi. "We've got to defeat them. Otherwise, you might as well bid the world farewell."

"And if the situation is resolved peacefully?"

"God forbid!" bellowed the bleary-eyed old man.

Then, as if to furnish proof of God's power, he added, "God is great! Would you believe I did it with my wife twice last night?"

"Twice!" exclaimed Husni Higgawi in amazement.

"I swear by the Book of God!"

"Bravo . . . bravo, Ashmawi!"

"So then, never despair of God's mercy!"

With a loud chortle, he looked over at Abduh Badran, who bowed his head in affirmation.

Then Ashmawi continued, "Why did what happened happen? It happened because we've lost religion and morals!"

But what are morals, thought Husni to himself. Your real crisis is that you're in need of new morals!

7

The street corner in front of L'Américaine coffeeshop was so crowded, there was nowhere to put one's feet. The young people were standing so close to each other that passersby were trapped between their warm youthful bodies. There was little or no conversation; eyes stared intently, and some moved their legs in subtle dance steps. Someone passing through the press of the crowd with his family, apparently irate over this affront to his dignity, shouted, "You should be ashamed of yourselves! If you're real men, go to the front!"

No one appeared to be ashamed of himself, and a voice shouted back, "Why does he want to send us to the front before it's time?"

Another voice shouted sarcastically, "Maybe he thinks they send women and middle-aged men!"

One group, weary of standing, withdrew and went over to the Geneva tavern. Congregating around a few bottles of beer, they started drinking and talking, for the most part without order or control. However, Marzouq Anwar took over the task of filling the glasses and passing them around.

"The problem of sex in . . . ."

"On the front there's a more important problem," someone interrupted.

"I'm just talking about domestic problems."

"Let him speak. Interrupting isn't allowed."

"An old-timer was talking to me once, and he told me that in his day, there was legalized prostitution."

"Our day is better, since sex is now like air and water!"

"Water doesn't reach the upper floors."

"But it does reach the lower floors!"

"It isn't like air and water, since girls have learned how to exploit it."

"It's a necessity of the age."

"Cars mean the downfall of innocence, for example."

"But there are always opportunities."

"There are buses, too."

"And the three o'clock parties at the movie theater."

"That doesn't matter. What matters is whether God exists!"

"And why do you want to know?"

"The only thing we used to worry about was Arab and African unity."

"What does that have to do with the existence of God?"

"The only thing we worry about now is when and how we can overcome the effects of the Tripartite Aggression."

"I've only got a minute. Does He exist, or doesn't He?"

"Those were glorious days."

"They were a dream."

"They were an illusion."

"And they get upset about us standing at the corner for a few minutes!"

"The dogs!"

"If the Jews are destined to leave, then who besides us is going to drive them out?"

"Who besides us is killed every day?"

"Who was killed in 1956? Who was killed in Yemen? Who was killed in 1967?"

"The old man thinks that having a half-naked girl at his disposal is everything."

"We've got to start from scratch."

". . . to get the nightmares off our chests."

"Nobody wants to answer my question. Does He exist?"

"All right, brother. If we judge by the chaos we see everywhere, then He couldn't possibly exist!"

"Isn't it possible that He owns the universe, but doesn't govern it?"

"If even unruly Egyptians are God's servants, then He *must* rule the universe!"

"Are you really planning to get married?"

"Yeah. Take your glass."

"Why?"

"Because I'm in love."

"What's this got to do with that?"

"We've got to do something, anyway."

"How do you explain the fact that more people are getting

married young?"

"Poverty!"

"Death!"

"The regime!"

"It's going to get so crowded, there won't be any room to sit down."

"Isn't it better to emigrate than to get married?"

"Marriage is a kind of internal emigration."

"The fact is, we need a little of the older generations' opportunism."

"You can't do without it in the crowd."

"So why is the world afraid of war?"

"War isn't the most terrible thing that threatens the world."

"Is there anything more terrible?"

"The individual isn't completely safe among his family. The family is afraid of the neighbors. The homeland is threatened by other nations. The world is surrounded by a hidden realm of dangerous creatures. The earth might be destroyed by a malfunction in the solar system, and the solar system might blow up and disappear in seconds."

"You're out of your mind!"

"But we've got to laugh and not let anything spoil our precious lives."

"Amen!"

"Amen!"

"Amen!"

8

Ashmawi's face had taken on a curious expression. His features bespoke an ominous, steely rage that had spread over the dryness of old age, the protruding jawbones and the sagging jowls, and when he received Husni Higgawi, there wasn't a trace of cheer in his countenance. Fearing some unnamed calamity, Husni turned to Amm Abduh as he took his seat, saying, "Everything's all right, I hope!"

When Ashmawi heard him, he approached until the two men were standing face to face. Then he began to spout.

"Curses on everything, and more than anything else, curses on me! I've declared a revolt against my weakness, my helplessness, and the way I've been thrown onto the scrap pile like some useless rag. Who am I? I'm Ashmawi the thug, the one with the iron fist and the blood-stained cudgel. There was a time when, at the mention of my name, men would tremble, women would run for cover, and policemen would pray to God for protection from me. I'm the ruthless, invincible criminal, the bloodthirsty despot, the Nimrod, the devil!"

Then he began to gasp.

In an indulgent, jocular tone, Husni Higgawi asked, "How can you complain of weakness when you're all of that?!"

"I'm talking about the past. It's about the past that I'm talking, not the present. Understand me well, sir. I was Darb al-Hilla's man, its protector, and woe betide anybody who hurt any of its residents. Thanks to me, they enjoyed peace and safety. Thanks to me, they could do whatever they wanted to others without fearing the consequences. My name was law, a sword, a blessing. It was riches; it was poverty. So what happened on the day when some despicable coward from the Qubaysi district assaulted a man from our neighborhood? I attacked that place as if God Almighty had destined it for destruction. I made no distinction between the accused and the innocent. Blows descended on the heads of passersby. I demolished corner stores, handcarts went up in flames, rocks rained down on windows and doors. Ask about me during the days of Saad Zaghloul, but don't ask about the number of my victims. From the time I slit an Englishman's throat and drank his blood, I was known as the 'the blood drinker.' That's Ashmawi the thug!"

Cursing him in his heart, Husni Higgawi said, "Your history's well-known, Ashmawi. But why are you so angry?"

The old man made no reply. Instead, he went back to where he'd been sitting near the door and immersed himself anew in sorrow and silence. Husni Higgawi looked over inquisitively at Amm Abduh.

With an apprehension bordering on fear, Amm Abduh said, "Two young men from Darb al-Hilla have been wounded."

"I thought the days of bullies and battles were gone for good!" Husni retorted reproachfully.

"They were wounded on the front."

At this Husni Higgawi fell into a gloomy silence, trying to think of something fitting to say.

But before he could say anything Ashmawi shouted, "The grandmother of one of them came to me, begging me to help the way I used to do in the old days! The old woman thought that Ashmawi was still the same as ever, somebody people could call on for help and who would rush to the rescue!"

"They're heroes, Ashmawi," said Husni Higgawi.

"You haven't seen them or the hospital ward they're in, then," the man said heatedly.

"You visited them in the hospital?"

"Yes, I did. I saw, and heard, and felt my helplessness. And I cursed everything, including myself."

Addressing himself primarily to Amm Abduh, Husni said sanguinely, "They're heroes. This is the way war goes, in all times and places."

"Curses on helplessness!" roared Ashmawi.

"Everything will be all right, God willing."

Trying to dispel his own fears with a bit of humor, Amm

Abduh said, "And you, Ashmawi, aren't you always calling for war and victory?"

His anger giving way to sadness, he repeated, "War and victory . . . but I'm just a useless old man!"

"It's enough that you drank that Englishman's blood when you were a young man."

Then Amm Abduh looked over at Husni Higgawi and said, "During the first revolution I was too young to fight, and now I'm too old. So I haven't done anything worth mentioning for my country."

"But your son is on the front. Tell me, does it pain you to think that you haven't done anything?"

"Sometimes. On the other hand, life's burdens are almost too much for me."

Husni recalled the fact that he was in a similar position, and that he used to go through crises of conscience in which he would take himself to task for not having done more for his country. However, he would quench the fires of conscience with the force of cold logic. In fact, he'd nearly convinced himself that he was using his apartment for innocent celebrations and charitable work.

"How will the situation end, sir?" Abduh Badran asked him.

"The eternal question!" replied Husni with a guffaw. "What can one say? We'll just have to wait . . . ."

"But death doesn't wait."

"It's a race, and we don't die alone!"

"Do rich people's sons get killed, too?" Ashmawi wondered aloud.

Unable to suppress a chuckle, Husni replied, "The draft makes no distinction between rich and poor, Ashmawi!"

"But do they really send them to the front?" he asked with a skeptical shake of the head. "I have a feeling they don't."

"Don't set so much store by your feelings, Ashmawi."

Turning his attention back to the shisha, Husni thought to himself: Tonight's session lacks its usual tranquility, and its laughter is tinged with grief. After all, defeat is a bitter pill to swallow. Its effects might shift from one center of the brain to another, but they can never be erased. A lofty mountain has disintegrated, and a wonderful dream has dissipated into thin air. The best thing I can do for myself is to leave the responsibility to those who are already bearing it.

As he exhaled the smoke through his mouth and nostrils, he asked himself: Where can I find a place where there's no mention of war?

9

The three young women—Aliyat Abduh, Saniya Anwar, and Mona Zahran, who'd been close friends since high school days—met on a balcony overlooking the Nile. There was a pleasant autumn chill in the air, and snow-white clouds adorned the late afternoon sky. Aliyat and Saniya had received a hurried invitation to Mona's house in Manyal, and they'd come expecting to hear happy news.

Mona was distinguished by a pristine beauty that revealed itself in her fair complexion, her striking black eyes, and her tallish, willowy frame. Another of her distinguishing features was her wealthy middle-class family. Her father was head of a law office and her mother was a school principal who had retired of her own accord and who had worked for the past year in the Ministry of Tourism. Mona had two brothers, one of them an engineer on a mission to the Soviet Union and the other a physician in al-Munufiya who expected to be sent abroad soon. Consequently, she was ambitious and a bit of a dreamer who didn't settle down easily. Despite the obvious differences between them, Mona's house reminded Aliyat and Saniya of Husni Higgawi's apartment. However, it had never occurred to them to feel envious of her thanks to the warm, intimate bond between them.

They had anticipated glad tidings from Mona. Instead, she said with a poignant curtness, "My engagement was broken before it was announced!"

The two girls were genuinely distressed.

"What?!" Saniya exclaimed.

"Unbelievable!" added Aliyat.

A month earlier at Dar al-Shay al-Hindi, Mona had introduced them to a young man by the name of Salim Ali, a judge at the Supreme Administrative Court, as a friend and prospective fiancé. Consequently, when they received Mona's hurried invitation, they'd expected something other than this distressing piece of news.

Shaking her head knowingly, Saniya said, "You're the one who broke it off, of course!"

"You always think the best of me!" replied Mona.

"But he's a nice-looking guy with a good position, Mona!"

Aliyat added, "And it was obvious that he loved you and that you felt the same way toward him!"

At this point Mona shifted uneasily in her chair, perhaps in response to some emotion she hadn't yet been able to uproot from her heart of hearts. Her two friends could see that the reason she had invited them was her need for companionship and consolation.

With a touch of sharpness in her voice she said, "I found out from a reliable source that he'd been making inquiries about me!"

Silence reigned until Saniya spoke up, saying, "Is that what you've got against him?"

"That's reason enough and more for me to be angry with him!"

"I'll bet he did it with good intentions!" said Aliyat.

"I'm not accusing him of bad intentions. I'm accusing him of a bad mentality."

Then she went on distraughtly, "I accused him to his face. He started hemming and hawing and tried to justify what he'd done by lying about his real motives. But I rejected the reasons he gave and told him to show some self-respect. He confessed to what he'd done and although he apologized, he made silly excuses that I don't remember and don't want to remember, and I didn't accept his apology. I said to him, 'Why don't you trying getting married through a matchmaker?' I asked him what he wanted to know about me that he didn't know already or that he couldn't find out through direct contact and his so-called love for me. He said he was innocent and that he did love me, and that my reputation was pure as driven snow. As for me, I sneered and told him I despised his inquiries and the results he'd arrived at, and that either he'd been deceived or hadn't investigated well enough. I told him, 'Just as your past is your business, my past is my business. I reject any kind of slavery, however it happens to disguise itself and whatever name it goes by.' And I told him he wasn't right for me and that I wasn't right for him."

Breathless, she fell silent, her eyes flashing and her lips quivering with rage. Her two friends appeared not to agree with the position she'd taken even though they shared her feelings and point of view.

"Don't you think you're going too far, Mona?" Aliyat asked her.

"After all," Saniya added, "this is the tradition in our country!"

Shaking her head obstinately, Mona replied, "I reject all of that."

"Men are hung up," Saniya said, "and they need to be broken in slowly."

Then, as if to complete Saniya's statement, Aliyat chimed in, "Not to be confronted."

Mona retorted superciliously, "I'd rather stay single if the price you have to pay for marriage is a silly lie and a shameful operation!"

"But our circumstances are delicate, as you know," Aliyat reminded her.

"I can't compromise my morals and principles," she said.

Indeed, Mona was well known for her moral standards. She'd only had sex for love. And unlike her two friends, she hadn't been obliged to do it over and over again in exchange for clothing, accessories, and books she needed. She may have frowned on their behavior. But even if she did, she sympathized with them from the bottom of her loving heart. She'd kept abreast of all the developments relating to their engagements, including the requisite forged statements, lies, and the rest. She hadn't been comfortable with a bit of it, but she consoled herself with the thought that all these absurdities were being committed in the name of true love.

Given what they knew of her stubbornness, pride, and idealism, they could see that their attempts to talk her out of her decision were doomed to failure. Hence, they resigned themselves gloomily to the reality of things.

"Mona," Aliyat told her, "you're a wonderful, beautiful girl, and you truly deserve a happy marriage."

"Are you two really confident of a future based on a huge lie?"

"It's based on love," replied Saniya.

As for Aliyat, her voice betrayed some apprehension when she said, "A man like Husni Higgawi can be trusted to keep our secret."

"I agree," said Mona, "we wouldn't expect him to betray us."

"Sometimes I think of the frightful coincidences in movies that turn everything upside down!" said Aliyat.

To this Saniya rejoined with a defiant strength, "We had no choice but to do what we did. And now we've got to accept our fates."

The visit stirred up whirlwinds of angst for Aliyat and Saniya. In the end, however, they knew deep down that what Saniya had said was a certainty: "We've got to accept our fates."

10

The triumph of her pride brought Mona no satisfaction, or at least, not the satisfaction she'd expected. At times when she was alone with herself, depression would sweep over her like gusts of dust-laden desert air. She feared she might go on doing one stupid thing after another. To her mutinous self she confessed that she still loved Salim despite his foolishness and stupidities. She could see that she had a problem and that it called for a solution.

Her brother, Dr. Ali Zahran, was visiting Cairo on vacation. Having him around was a solace to her, and she told him about her failed relationship. Yet as sorry as he was to hear her story, there were other concerns foremost in his mind.

"I'm thinking of emigrating!" he told her.

"Emigrating!" she murmured in astonishment.

"The fact is, I'm past the thinking stage, and I've made up my mind to do it."

"But haven't you been waiting to be sent abroad on a medical mission?"

"I just keep getting put off. So I started to think of emigrating, and then I decided it was the thing to do."

"How will you manage it?"

"I'm about to finish up my research on parasites, and once it's ready, I'll send it to a colleague of mine who's emigrated to the United States for him to present it to universities and medical centers there. Then I'll wait for an invitation to work at one of them. At least, that's the way things happened with him."

She drew in her breath with excitement.

"I'll go with you!" she said. Then she added confidently, "I'm a specialist in statistics, and my English is good."

"It would be better for us to emigrate together than for me to emigrate alone," he said with a smile.

Their parents objected to the idea. To them it made no sense given the fact that both Mona and her brother had promising futures in Egypt.

"The country's become disgusting," the doctor told his parents.

"It's unbearable," Mona chimed in.

The father tried to stir up their patriotic sentiments. However, with a boldness that struck his father as cruel, Dr. Ali said, "A homeland isn't just land and geographical borders anymore. It's a place where you belong intellectually and spiritually!"

Dr. Ali's words pained his father, who belonged to the 1919 generation, the generation of pure Egyptian nationalism. He found it disturbing to listen to his son, and he felt as though he were witnessing a strange new phenomenon that was impossible to understand or explain. He was resigned to the fact that he couldn't dissuade his children from something they'd set their minds to, and he wondered in anguish how he would be able to endure life without them by his side, or at least in the same country. Mona loved her father very much even though they hardly agreed on anything. She marveled at the way the June 5 defeat had brought his patriotism to the surface anew and infused it with new life, whereas in her case, it had so completely disillusioned her that she felt compelled to keep changing her skin one cell at a time. This was what had happened to Aliyat, Saniya, and others, and to her brother as well.

"We're living without a purpose," she said to him.

"And I'm living without a life," he replied ruefully.

"We've got to emigrate."

"We'll leave at the earliest opportunity."

Mona had come to think of herself as a tourist in her own country, and she felt a relief she hadn't experienced since the time when she broke up with Salim Ali. It wasn't long before the news had gotten around to her friends and colleagues and in the circles in which she moved. She took to dreaming of a new, pristine life that provided people with the means to achieve progress, prosperity, and security.

Then one day as she was on her way home from her office, whom should she find before her but Salim Ali in Talaat Harb Square. It wasn't a coincidence, nor did he try to claim that it was. Holding out his hand to her, he said, "I heard you were emigrating to the United States, and I couldn't bear not to say goodbye."

She shook his hand with a frostiness that concealed her agitation.

"Thank you," she said.

She kept on walking and he walked along beside her. She cast him a look of protest which he ignored.

"I said, 'Thank you!'" she repeated.

"But I'm not going to leave you," he replied calmly.

"Why not?" she asked with the same frostiness with which she'd shaken his hand.

As if he were confessing to a crime, he replied guiltily, "It's become clear to me that I love you, and that I haven't been able to give you up."

Scandalously happy over what he'd said, she lowered her gaze as she said, "As for me, I've been able to give you up."

"So then," he said, unfazed, "let's go to Dar al-Shay al-Hindi."

They walked along side by side, her dreams now upside down.

"Love is the most important thing in the world!" he said, heaving a sigh of relief.

Then, with an even greater relief that bespoke the torment he had endured, he continued, "It really is. Love is the most important thing in the world. Everything else is a lie."

Looking at her inquisitively, he said, "Are you really going to emigrate?"

"Yes," she replied halfheartedly.

"I wish I could emigrate too."

"What's stopping you?" she asked with a smile.

"My specialty doesn't qualify me." Then he added with a chuckle, "I'll just have to stay put in this madhouse."

11

Through a single decree, Marzouq Anwar and his fiancée Aliyat Abduh had become government employees. She'd been appointed to the Ministry of Social Affairs, and he to the educational district in Beni Sueif. The excitement over their appointments was dampened by Marzouq's prospective locale, and their impending separation hung like a pall over the two young lovers. They wondered: How can a newlywed couple be together with one of them in Cairo and the other in Beni Sueif?

Marzouq went to the Cairo train station accompanied by his father and Aliyat, and the three of them sat around a table in the canteen until it was time for the train to Upper Egypt to depart. Marzouq's father was sixty, though he looked at least ten years older than his age. He was the type that takes things with ease and resignation. Besides, he considered his son to be among "the lost" in any case, regardless of whether he stayed in Cairo or went to Aswan. Consequently, he'd always encouraged him. He cited an example for him from his own life during the 1930s—the years of the economic crisis— at which time he'd been shunted back and forth between the countries of the region, merchants were haunted by the specter of bankruptcy, and businesses were being liquidated right and left.

Just then Aliyat leaned over and asked Marzouq, "Do you know that man sitting across from us?"

He looked over and saw a man seated a short distance away. He was smoking a pipe and scrutinizing him with an uninhibited, penetrating gaze.

"No," he replied without hesitation.

He didn't know him, though he looked vaguely familiar. Where had he seen that plump, squarish face before, with its luminous eyes and bushy eyebrows and that imposing bald head?

"He hasn't taken his eyes off you since we got here," Aliyat said in a whisper.

Surely, he thought, the man would take his eyes off him now that they'd become aware of his gaze. However, not content with just looking, he calmly got up and, before they knew it, was standing at their table.

Bowing his head in greeting, he introduced himself, saying, "Muhammad Rashwan, film director."

Marzouq Anwar rose and, bowing his head in turn, said, "Marzouq Anwar, government employee. Pleased to meet you, sir."

Continuing to look him over, the man said, "Do you have any acting experience?"

"No." Marzouq replied, taken aback.

"Wouldn't you like to try your hand at it?"

Laughing in spite of his tense nerves, Marzouq said, "It had never occurred to me."

With a knowing nod of the head the man said, "I've got a leading role for you."

"A leading role!" Marzouq exclaimed in astonishment.

"I'd been worried about whether I was going to find someone to fill the part, but when I took a look at you, I knew I'd found what I was looking for. So, what do you say?"

His voice trembling, Marzouq said, "Give me a little time."

"He's on his way to start a new job!" his father interjected.

"If he takes this role, will it guarantee steady work for him?" Aliyat queried.

"I have more than one leading role for him, and I predict that he'll be a success."

"But he's never acted before," she objected.

"That's better, in fact. After he's trained with me, he'll turn out polished and perfect."

His head spinning, Marzouq announced his decision.

"I'll do it," he said.

"Think it over a little first, son."

"I'll do it," he repeated resolutely. "I'm going to try my luck."

Muhammad Rashwan gave him his card, saying, "Meet me at 10 o'clock tomorrow morning at this address. Do you have a telephone?"

Marzouq shook his head.

"Your role is a new one, actually: a young university graduate who's been drafted, and who then visits Cairo on a brief leave of absence. While he's there, big things happen in his life, and a woman of unknown nationality falls in love with him and invites him to run away with her."

"Does he actually run away with her?" Marzouq asked.

"That question is answered in the movie. The important thing is for conditions to remain the way they are until it comes out."

"What conditions do you mean?"

"I mean the situation on the front."

"Do you expect it to change before then?"

"The producer is convinced that things are going to stay the way they are for years. If, on the other hand . . . ."

"If . . . ?" Marzouq probed.

Laughing, Muhammad Rashwan went on, "If we're defeated again, or even if we win, it will spell disaster for the movie and the people making it!"

12

Marzouq Anwar came out clad in his military uniform, his eyes exuding a boyish innocence. He met with the woman of unknown nationality who, unbeknownst to him, was hot on his trail while feigning nonchalance. She asked him a passing question. He replied politely and initially without interest. Then suddenly, drawn by her dazzling beauty, he was swept off his feet.

Behind the camera, in the midst of a cluster of viewers, stood Aliyat Abduh, Saniya Anwar, Mona Zahran, Ibrahim Abduh, and Salim Ali. Those looking on even had to breathe with the greatest of care, as total silence was the order of the day. The only place life stirred was beneath the camera's bright lights. When Muhammad Rashwan announced that the take was over, the two actors came out of their roles and those standing behind the camera were resurrected to new life.

"He's a natural!" commented Mona.

"It's incredible!" seconded Ibrahim.

In vain Aliyat tried to conceal her nervousness and the excitement she felt in her heart. Marzouq came up to them and shook their hands. Then he embraced Ibrahim, and the two of them stood there grinning at each other in their identical military attire.

Addressing her brother Ibrahim, Aliyat said, "He's playing you in the film!"

After giving him a careful inspection, Ibrahim said, "You look smart as an officer."

"That's because he's making love, not war!" said Saniya with a laugh.

"Does your role take you to the front?" Ibrahim asked him.

"Yes," Marzouq replied. "I read it in the script, and it depicts superhuman heroism."

Ibrahim laughed but didn't say a word. The director Muhammad Rashwan came out and shook hands with everyone. He had met Aliyat and Saniya before, and was now introduced to Mona Zahran and her fiancé, Salim Ali. He inspected people's faces the way a goldsmith inspects pieces of jewelry.

He came up to Ibrahim and said, "We'll be needing you for some key information."

"For some secrets, you mean?" Ibrahim laughed.

"No. We just need to know what sorts of things are permissible to film."

"Not everything that's permissible to film is advisable to film!"

"Our purpose is simply to salute your heroism," Muhammad Rashwan assured him. Turning to Mona Zahran he asked, "Don't you agree to that?"

She nodded.

Then, turning back to Ibrahim, "All of us are soldiers, but in different fields."

"Maybe," replied Ibrahim coolly, "but we're fighting, and you're acting."

Everyone laughed.

It was nearly time for them to shoot a new scene, so Marzouq and Muhammad Rashwan took leave of the group.

Once they were gone, Mona said, "That director doesn't inspire confidence."

"But he's incredibly perceptive, and he's extremely good at what he does," Aliyat offered in his defense.

Curling her lips, Mona said, "Unlike many, I have great respect for comedies."

"Why's that, sweetheart?" Salim Ali asked her.

"Well, at least they're honest!"

"You're right," replied Ibrahim, laughing in pure merriment for the first time.

Then he whispered in Saniya's ear, "I nearly got killed twice yesterday!"

"God forbid!" she whispered back, grasping his hand tenderly. A somber look flashed across her green eyes.

"When are you planning to emigrate?" Aliyat asked Mona playfully.

"The project fell through," Mona replied. Then, pointing to Salim Ali, she added, "And it's all this guy's fault!"

"We owe you a word of thanks, then," Aliyat said to Salim.

"In any case, it's a way of emulating the Prophet to emigrate," Mona remarked.

"Even if it's to the United States?" Ibrahim asked.

"Even if it's to hell!" she retorted defiantly.

13

In a hurriedly arranged visit, Aliyat and Saniya met Mona Zahran at her home in Manyal. It wasn't an ordinary visit, or at least, this is what Mona gathered from the look in her friends' eyes.

"We have an important message for you," announced Aliyat.

Mona's curiosity was piqued to the hilt.

"What message?" she asked. "From whom?"

"From Marzouq Anwar!"

"The famous actor?"

"The film director Muhammad Rashwan would like a private interview with you," Saniya told her.

Her eyes wide with astonishment, Mona didn't know what to say.

"He's opening up to you the world of stardom!" said Aliyat.

"And if you want to know the truth," added Saniya, "you seem cut out for it."

Excited, Mona thought for a bit, then murmured, "It had never even crossed my mind."

"It had never crossed Marzouq's mind, either," Aliyat said.

"I'd like to know what the two of you think about it."

"Try your luck without hesitation," Aliyat told her.

"Without hesitation!" affirmed Saniya.

"But I've never tried acting before."

"You might try something because you love it, or you might come to love it after you try it. It's all the same in the end."

During the few hours that followed the friends' get-together, Mona began thinking the matter over, and before long the idea had taken hold of her and she'd fallen captive to its magic. She phoned Salim Ali and asked him to meet her at Dar al-Shay al-Hindi. When she told him what she'd decided to do, the young man was stunned and bewildered.

"This has got to be a joke!" he said.

"I mean exactly what I say," she assured him.

"You, a movie star!" he cried in anguish.

She furrowed her brow. "And why not?"

"No!" he said furiously.

She didn't like his tone of voice. As for him, he was incensed by her self-importance.

"I won't let you talk to me this way!" she said.

"And I refuse to be scandalized!"

"Scandalized! You . . . you . . . ."

Interrupting her heatedly, he said, "I've put up with enough on your account, and this is as far as I can go!"

"So you think you've got me in your debt, do you?" she shouted.

"I meant exactly what I said."

Her face pallid with agitation, she said, "That's it. That's it. I never want to see your face again!"

He got up from the table, saying, "You're hung up and out of your mind!"

And thus their engagement was broken for the second time.

In part because she was so distraught, and in part because it was what she had wanted to do all along, Mona sought out an interview with Muhammad Rashwan. When she went to visit him with Marzouq Anwar in his office on Urabi Street, he welcomed her warmly, then sat down at his desk, saying, "Miss Mona, I've discovered so much new talent that people call me 'Columbus,' and never once have my expectations been disappointed. So consider yourself a success from this very moment."

Pointing to Muhammad Rashwan, Marzouq said to her, "I believe in this man!"

Muhammad Rashwan then went on to say, "I nominate you for the leading role in a movie I'm quite proud of. Do you sing?"

"No," she replied diffidently.

"That doesn't matter. We can do without the singing. However, I won't be free to start work on the new film for six more months."

"That will give us time to do the necessary tests and promotion," offered Marzouq.

"Bravo, Marzouq. So, then, everything's been agreed on."

Two days after the interview, the director called Mona and asked her to come to his office. In this one-on-one meeting, he took some photographs of her and conducted some voice tests. He also invited her to act out a dramatic situation from one of his movies. He encouraged her the entire time with a charming smile. As a result, she warmed to him, and her heart fluttered with gratitude. At the same time, she wasn't pleased with the test results despite his friendly encouragement. She was inclined to believe that she wasn't cut out for this particular art form, and that any effort she made in this area would be a waste.

Confiding her fears to him one day, she said, "I'm not happy with myself."

"That's exactly what Fitna Nadir said about herself after her first test."

Feeling a bit hopeful, she smiled sweetly.

"Fitna Nadir was originally a university graduate like you, and she's now a precious jewel in the world of dramatic art!"

There followed a series of additional meetings and tests, though most of the time was spent in general conversation about art and life. Mona noticed that his thinking tended to be unsophisticated despite his fame and success, and that one might have found him pleasant enough company were it not for his intolerable conceit and class consciousness. Another thing she noticed was that he was more taken with her than he was with her acting ability. In fact, she'd come to the conclusion that he wasn't the slightest bit interested in her as an actress, and that the whole thing was nothing but a trap. From that time on, clouds of resentment, rage, and disappointment began to gather ominously in her heart.

One day, thinking that the time had come to reap the fruits of his labors, he said to her, "The office isn't the right place for such pleasant conversations. What do we say we go out for dinner?"

Realizing what was behind his words, she started to feel sick to her stomach.

"You'll have to see my cozy little nest in 'Amiriya!" he added.

Feeling his tobacco-saturated breath on her cheek, she lost her temper and slapped him in the face.

He lurched backward until he'd regained his balance, his eyes like stone and his cheeks swollen with rage, and before she knew it he'd come down on her cheek with the palm of his rough hand. Reeling from the blow, she fell to the floor.

"So, you think you're a woman who shouldn't be touched according to the rules of modern propriety? You despicable ingrate."

Incredulous, she got to her feet, her hair disheveled and her head spinning.

"Get out of here, you whore," he bellowed, "and tell this story to your mother!"

Her head still spinning, she picked up her purse, straightened her hair, and headed for the door.

Meanwhile, his voice followed her, "My dinner invitation still stands. And say hello to your mother for me!"

14

Salim Ali had declared an all-out revolt. He'd made up his mind to spurn Mona and show her nothing but contempt. He considered her mad, and that it was a lucky thing he'd seen her for what she really was before getting mixed up in a marriage to her.

Dubious of his so-called revolt, his younger brother Hamid said to him, "You're still in love with her, brother."

"No, I'm not!" he shouted angrily. "You'll see for yourself!"

Hamid loved his brother and believed that he understood him.

"You're bourgeois, brother, and a bourgeois marriage suits you!"

Angrier than ever now, Salim retorted, "You and your jargon! Just wait. You'll see . . . ."

"And your legal position . . ." Hamid said with a note of concern in his voice.

"You wait and see," Salim interrupted.

Returning to an old haunt that he had abandoned from the time he'd met Mona Zahran, he went half-drunk to the Markib al-Shams nightclub in the Haram district. Withdrawing into the club's outside seating area despite the cold weather, he asked the waiter to call Samira to come drink with him. His friend Samira was a fourth-class dancer who danced together with a group at the back of the stage when a singer was performing at the nightclub. Thirty-five years old and on the cheap side, she had a touch of beauty, though her body was more beautiful than her face.

Surprised to see him back after an absence of more than six months, she pretended to be angry for no real reason and said to him, "So, you're back, traitor!"

They started drinking, and she noted that unlike usual, he was drinking heavily. She had always liked him because he was well-mannered, because he had a small car, and lastly, because he was generous.

"You're drinking like a fiend!" she said with a giggle.

"I'll be waiting for you later tonight," he said.

Deep down she welcomed his words. However, wanting to teach him a lesson, she said, "No!"

They exchanged a long look.

"I've got other plans tonight," she said.

"No, you don't!" he cried grumpily.

"No!"

"How's your little girl?"

"She's with my mother, as you know."

He downed his glass, then said, "I've got a good idea."

"An idea?"

He hesitated a bit since he was aware, despite his drunken state, that he was about to take the most serious step he'd ever taken in his life.

Angry at his hesitation, he said, "Samira, I want us to live together."

She thought a bit, then murmured, "There are two ways of looking at it!"

"But you don't understand what I mean."

"I think it's obvious."

Staring intently at his glass, he said, "I want to marry you!"

She looked at him incredulously.

"You're drunk!" she said testily.

"On the contrary, that's why I came back."

Now she started eyeing him suspiciously.

"What do you say?" he asked.

"Sober up!"

"Tonight, if possible!"

Then, taking her hand, he went on, "The little girl will stay with your mother. However, I'll arrange a reasonable income for her. I'm not rich, and I'm not poor."

"So you're really serious?!" she asked in amazement.

"Come on, we can do it right now if you want."

"What made you decide to do this?" she asked with an embarrassed laugh.

"I want to settle down. I want to settle down with a sensible woman without deceit. So, are you ready to forget the past and start a new life?"

She laughed nervously and said, "No justice of the peace would be awake at this hour of the night."

"That's all right, as long as he'll be waking up early in the morning."

15

Dr. Ali Zahran gazed sadly over at his sister Mona. He was boiling with rage on the inside, but all that showed on his face was grief.

"Mona," he said, "you're a wonderful girl, and I can't imagine such a thing . . . ."

"Just forget all about it," she said ruefully.

"But I can feel that slap on my own face!"

"Tell me about the emigration project."

"Emigration!" Then he added unenthusiastically, "The procedures take a long time, but I'm waiting."

"I don't want to stay in this country one more day."

Still seething inside, he said, "The trouble with you is that you're too sensitive. You shouldn't have broken up with a man like Salim Ali in a moment of anger."

"I don't want to stay in this country one more day," she said tearfully.

"He's a great guy, and he loves you."

"Let's get off that subject."

"Sometimes I wonder why it is that we always think we're right."

"Because we are!" she said with a grin.

"The defeat has shaken us up."

"And enlightened us."

"Would you allow me to contact Salim Ali?"

"No!" she said, jumping up in a panic.

"Think it over a bit."

"No."

"Don't you want to—"

"I want to emigrate," she said vehemently.

He shrugged his shoulders, then bade her farewell and left the house. He went to a pharmacy and called Muhammad

Rashwan's office to inquire about his whereabouts, and was told that he was working at the Egypt Studio. He tried to call, but the line was busy, so he got into his car and went tearing off in the direction of the studio. When he arrived at 10:00 p.m., he learned that Muhammad Rashwan had left the studio, and an employee informed him that he had gone to the Jamaica Restaurant for dinner. So he headed his car in that direction along the desert road. Once there, he checked out the reception area and went wandering about the restaurant's open-air section, but he found no trace of him. The maitre d' told him that Muhammad Rashwan hadn't arrived yet, so he started pacing back and forth in front of the restaurant. Finally, at around 11:00 p.m., a car pulled up in the parking lot. As two men got out, the doorman pointed to one of them and said to Dr. Ali, "That's Mr. Muhammad Rashwan."

Walking several steps ahead of Marzouq Anwar, he strutted forward at a calm, leisurely pace in his off-white leather jacket and his navy blue trousers. Dr. Ali Zahran approached him at a similar pace in the light of the two lamps that stood next to the entrance. The man looked nonchalantly in Dr. Ali's direction, perhaps expecting to hear a word of admiration or a suggestion of some sort relating to his work. However, without uttering a word, the doctor kicked him in the stomach with all the strength he could muster. Muhammad Rashwan let forth a moan that sounded like the lowing of a cow, and his eyes were fixed in a blank stare. Then he collapsed on his face. The whole thing happened with such lightning speed that Marzouq Anwar just stood aghast, frozen like a statue.

Once he'd wakened from his stupor, he screamed, "Are you out of your mind?"

The doorman came running and a few drivers gathered around. Some of them congregated around Dr. Ali, while others knelt around the fallen Muhammad Rashwan.

"I'm the brother of Mona Zahran, you bastard!" Dr. Ali Zahran bellowed at the man that lay sprawled before him.

Marzouq Anwar seized him by the neck. "You're crazy!" he screamed. "You'll never get away from me!"

Peeling Marzouq's hands off of him angrily, he screamed back, "He's a bastard who deserves to be taught a lesson!"

Then a voice rang out from among the people huddled over the man lying on the ground.

"He's dead. Arrest the murderer!"

16

Mona went with her father to the office of an attorney by the name of Hasan Hammouda on Sabri Abu Alam Street. Mr. Zahran had remembered him in his ordeal, not only on account of the fact that they had been colleagues for many years, but, in addition, because he believed him to be one of the three top criminal lawyers in the country. Hasan Hammouda's office was spacious and plush. A man of towering height with a dark complexion and scintillating eyes, he received them both, then turned to extend a special welcome to Mr. Zahran. His eyes rested in a near-trance on Mona for several seconds before he invited the two of them to sit down.

Mr. Zahran proceeded to tell his story. Soon, however, Hasan Hammouda interrupted him, saying, "So, the accused is your son? That possibility had never occurred to me!"

The man then went on with his story-turned-court-case, then concluded it with a sigh.

"And the rest is in the newspapers!" said Hasan Hammouda.

Then, looking at Mona admiringly, he added, "It's a regrettable thing that when someone who deserves to die is killed by someone without the proper qualifications, it's considered a crime!"

Sounding fragile and defeated, she said, "I never imagined it would end in tragedy!"

"Some tragedies are comprehensible, and some aren't."

"My brother's never been known to have aggressive tendencies."

"If he were experienced in aggression, he wouldn't have been implicated in an unintentional crime."

Then he asked her to tell the story with which the tragedy had begun, whereupon she related it to him in all its details.

"Were there witnesses?" he asked.

"We were alone in his office."

Then Mr. Zahran asked, "Is there any justification for making a false claim against him?"

"You know the intricacies of the law better than I do," replied Hasan Hammouda with a smile.

"It's obvious that he didn't mean to kill him," said Mona.

"I'll have to take a look at the case file first. However, what's been published in the newspapers indicates that the doctor had been seeking out a meeting with the victim, that he had looked for him in the Egypt Studio as well as at the Jamaica Restaurant, and that he had waited for him. Then what happened, happened."

"But is that enough to prove that it was premeditated murder?"

"No. But did he wound him in a vital part?"

"Even if he did, there's no doubt that it happened by accident."

"However, we're required to prove any point of view we propose. And don't forget that he's a physician. As such, in the view of the court, he's an expert in vital parts!"

A look of distress appeared in the girl's eyes, and he said benevolently, "But this is what our struggle will revolve around. We'll have to prove that he only intended to hit the man, and that it led accidentally to his death."

Falling to pieces completely now, she asked, "And hope? Isn't there any hope?"

"Of course there is!" he thundered. "There's a great deal of hope! And in God we trust!"

The days that followed were hell for Mona, and Aliyat and Saniya were almost constantly at her side.

She would say, "Even if he's acquitted of the charge of first-degree murder, his future is still down the drain."

There was nothing anyone could say to console her.

"Curses on me!" she cried. "Everything is my fault!"

She sought out an opportunity to visit her brother in prison, and when she saw him, she burst into bitter, hysterical tears.

But to her amazement, she found him calm and resigned to his fate.

"That's enough crying, Mona," he said. "It won't do any good."

"But it's all my damned fault!" she sobbed.

"You were attacked," he replied calmly. "It was only natural for you to confide in me how you felt, and it was only natural for me to be furious."

He muttered something under his breath, then said, "There's a senseless mistake here that I have no control over. The man was killed, and I'm done for."

"I'm the senseless mistake, Ali."

"It's bigger than both of us."

"If you only hadn't gotten so angry!"

"But I did," he said, exasperated, "and I have to accept my fate."

17

The film was assigned to the director Ahmad Ridwan, who took over the remaining stages of the filming while striving as far as possible to preserve Muhammad Rashwan's style. Marzouq Anwar won the new director's admiration to an extent he hadn't expected, and his hopes for the future were revived. Known in his field for the speed with which he got things done, the good quality of his work, and the popularity of his productions, Ahmad Ridwan was a successful director with a wealth of contacts. As a consequence, the doors of employment were opened to Marzouq.

Ahmad Ridwan said to him, "You're a gifted actor. I'm going to make you the true successor of Anwar Wagdi."

Elated, Marzouq began dreaming of future glory.

"But," he went on, "don't restrict yourself to a single style. Mastering a single style can be helpful, but flexibility is better in the long run. What I mean by flexibility is for you to be able to play roles that span the entire spectrum, from the hero to the villain. And in both cases, you've got the lead role." With a melancholy sigh he said, "That's not the way Muhammad Rashwan saw things."

He shook his head in regret, then added, "He was so kind, and he died such a senseless death! So, you say you know Mona, the murderer's sister?"

"Only superficially. But she's a friend of my sister and of my fiancée. Do you believe the claims she made when she was questioned?"

He shrugged, saying, "I've heard rumors that there was a sexual relationship between the murderer and the deceased."

Shocked, Marzouq replied, "But the deceased . . . I mean, I'd never heard that he . . . ."

"Never mind," Ahmad Ridwan interrupted. "The investigation will reveal the truth whatever it is. May he rest in peace. It isn't proper to speak ill of him now that he's gone to be with God!"

The two men were sitting in the studio cafeteria when, without requesting permission, a young woman came and sat down with them. Ahmad Ridwan introduced her to Marzouq, saying,

"Fitna Nadir, a new star like you. Only her rise to fame started a year ago."

Marzouq recognized her from her photographs. He had also been told by the late Muhammad Rashwan of her special relationship with Ahmad Ridwan. She was possessed of a distinctive beauty which, though one might not notice it at first glance, would pierce you to the core. It seemed to him that her features were somewhat out of proportion to each other. Nevertheless, she was overwhelmingly attractive. Her body was petite overall, but its contours were full, and she was svelte and exceedingly sensual. Ahmad Ridwan was fifty-five years old, with a daughter married to an employee in the diplomatic corps and a son who worked as an engineer on a mission to the Soviet Union. Hence, his passion was marked by the madness of middle age. As for Fitna, she was a university graduate and was known to be the paramour of a rich Arab by the name of Sheikh Yazid who had furnished an apartment for her on the twentieth floor of the Nile Building, but who only came to Cairo briefly or during specific seasons.

"Fitna is a rare talent, and you'll be working with her in the next film."

Patting her hand affectionately, he said to Marzouq, "She's the sister of an officer who was martyred in the June War."

When Marzouq's film was shown, it was a considerable success. As for him personally, he was acknowledged as a gifted artist, and more than one critic predicted that he would have a brilliant future.

Ahmad Ridwan contracted him for three films and he began to feel that he was finding his feet. Consequently, he made up his mind to marry Aliyat at the earliest opportunity.

When he shot the first movie with Fitna Nadir, he felt as though she was making him the object of special attention. However, he responded with the greatest of caution lest he do anything to disturb his good relations with Ahmad Ridwan.

One day as the two actors were taking a break in the studio garden between shootings, she asked him, "I hear you're getting married. Is that so?"

"As soon as possible," he replied good-naturedly.

"Congratulations in advance."

Then she added, "You'll be the first new actor who's married."

"That's right."

"But don't you need unrestricted freedom, especially at the start of your career?"

"It's already been a long engagement, and there's no good reason to put it off."

She fell silent for a while, giving herself over to the coolness of the night.

Then she asked him, "Is your fiancée an actress, too?"

"She and I were classmates at university, and now she works in the Ministry of Social Affairs."

"I think she'll need the wisdom of Socrates to be happy with you, then."

"What hyperbole!"

She walked away until she'd disappeared into the darkness. Then she came back into the light and said, "There's a chance for the two of us to establish a partnership."

"A partnership?" he said, bewildered.

"Not in the commercial sense. I mean a successful duo."

"I heard the same thing from Ahmad Ridwan, and I was pleased."

"So we should be enthusiastic about our duo!"

"I'm quite happy to do that."

"And I have complete confidence in Ahmad Ridwan's opinion."

She tossed him a violet that she had been twirling between her thumb and forefinger, then disappeared again. Marzouq was rattled. Engulfed by a happy, wicked sort of emotion, he thought remorsefully of Aliyat.

18

Husni Higgawi seemed more serious than usual. He stood in the sitting room looking apprehensively at Mona Zahran. She didn't return his glances. Her black eyes half-closed and her countenance grave, she leaned back into the large armchair as though she were asleep.

He said to himself: She's the only woman friend who never went along with my caprices. The only thing she'll surrender to is love. He recalled the way she had come to visit him for the first time as a university student. She had come out of curiosity with Aliyat and Saniya and had watched his pornographic films, but without slipping despite the arousal they could provoke. She had never given him anything but friendship, and long ago he had ceased asking for anything more from her.

"I invited you because I had a feeling you needed a friend in your time of trial."

A feeble smile of gratitude creased her lips.

"I've invited you before, but you didn't come!" he continued.

"I was in too much grief."

Leaning toward her, he said tenderly, "In any case, be thankful to God. Hasan Hammouda is a capable lawyer, and he saved his neck from the noose."

Ruefully she replied, "But he'll spend ten years in prison, and he's lost his future forever!"

"It's still a lighter sentence than he might have gotten."

"And I'm the real criminal!"

"What could you have done? All you did was confide your concern to your brother."

"What you're saying isn't going to make me feel any less guilty."

The man lifted the glass in his hand to his lips, then looked over at the glass that sat near her hand on the arm of the easy chair, as though inviting her to take a drink. He took a few steps back and leaned on the edge of the bar. Then he said, "Think about the worries of people around us, and your own worries won't look so bad."

"I doubt it."

"So, then," he asked with a smile, "you're determined to be depressed?"

"I'm not depressed. I'm living my life, but it has no taste."

Nodding his huge head, he said, "I might feel depressed now and then. But do you know how I deal with it? I remember the thousands of people who've been killed and the possibilities still in store for us, and it isn't long before my own unhappiness seems of less account."

She shrugged sullenly and didn't say a word.

He went on, "I was really shaken up by the student revolution. Then I remembered that we might be buried under the rubble at any moment."

"But there's something that's even worse," she cried with sudden vehemence, "that in reality we're living as beggars!"

Husni Higgawi bellowed with laughter as he said, "You hit the nail on the head!"

"Why do you laugh like that?"

"Believe me, I haven't laughed from my heart once since June 5!"

Then he added, "My dear Mona, it's nothing but sounds that come out of my mouth!"

"How can some people sleep so well?"

"They put on the magical spectacles of history and another vision comes into view."

"Don't those spectacles see tens of thousands of victims?"

"No. They see something worse."

"Are you serious?"

"Absolutely."

"So, then, you're satisfied?"

"I'm not a maker of history. So my vision might be clouded by grief and a sense of futility."

He turned his back to her to refill his glass. In the meantime, she took her glass and drank half. He turned toward her again, saying, "Drink some more. You need three glasses at least."

She smiled for the first time and said, "You're clearly patriotic in a sentimental sort of way. So, have you done your duty?"

He downed his drink in a single gulp, then said, "At my age, it's enough for me to take my camera and visit the front in order to have done my duty."

"Then you come home to your enchanted house."

"I latch onto ephemeral pleasures out of terror and sorrow."

"Happy are the middle-aged!"

"It's a miserable country whose middle-aged folks are envied for their middle age!"

They exchanged a long look that wasn't without a touch of sweetness.

Then he said, "I invited you here to provide you with some diversion, so look . . . ."

Interrupting him calmly, she said, "Hasan Hammouda wants to marry me."

Startled and perplexed, Husni Higgawi said nothing for quite some time.

Then he exclaimed, "The man's my age!"

"He's forty," she said, shaking her head.

"I bet you'll agree to it."

"Why do you think that?"

"You might do it in protest against the love that led you to give the most precious thing you had but gave you nothing except trouble."

"Salim Ali has married a prostitute!" she said scornfully.

"That word has no meaning anymore."

With a sigh she replied, "Isn't it ironic that two people should do to themselves what we've done even though they're in love with each other?"

"Finish your glass and marry Hasan Hammouda. There's no point in your staying alone and dwelling on your woes till they destroy you."

He talked to her at length about Hasan Hammouda, his well-established Upper Egyptian family, the land he owned that had been liquidated during the agricultural reform, and his genius as a lawyer.

Then he asked her, "Have you seen my most recent flicks?"

She laughed as he headed for the screening room.

19

It was after midnight at the Inshirah coffeeshop, but their session was a glum one that augured no good. Husni Higgawi smoked his shisha in total silence. He stole a glance at Abduh Badran only to find him lost in thought. Ashmawi squatted in the corner near the stove, drawing imaginary lines on the pavement with his finger. Husni Higgawi said to himself: It's a dreary night, and the nights to come will be bitter as gall.

Picking up on one of Husni Higgawi's glances, Abduh Badran said, "Just like that, the wedding's off!"

"It's just been postponed," Husni Higgawi said consolingly.

"I hope you're right!"

"God is great, Abduh."

"When he didn't come home at the time he'd been scheduled to, my heart started pounding like crazy. And before that his mother had had a terrible dream . . . ."

"It's nothing serious, I hope."

"How should I know? I was only allowed to visit him for a minute. And I couldn't see anything of him. His face, his head, and his neck were covered with gauze!"

"That's nothing but a routine medical procedure."

"And we were getting ready for his and his sister Aliyat's weddings," the man said with a sigh.

"In a week or a month they'll have their celebrations!"

Husni wondered to himself: Is this what happens to fathers and mothers everywhere? Are there other peoples who are truly steeped in the spirit of combat and freedom fighting? Has history so falsified its accounts of heroism that they haven't come down to us in the way they really happened? Is it a fault in us, or is this the way human nature has always been? And if so, then how has it been possible to lure human communities into one war after another? What a difference there is between the way sacrifice is portrayed in a daily newspaper, a history book, or a poem, and the way it comes across in a coffeeshop, a house, or a neighborhood! Nevertheless, there isn't an occupation on the face of the earth that people have engaged in against their wills the way they have in that of war.

Ashmawi lifted his head off his knees and said, "We're miserable down-and-outers, Mr. Husni."

Abduh Badran seconded the opinion, saying, "That's right. We're miserable down-and-outers."

"What can I say?" Husni replied. "If I were a young man, it would be my duty to be gung-ho for war!"

"A neighbor lady's son had to have his leg amputated," said Ashmawi.

"That's war for you, Ashmawi. And your country is occupied."

The old man said heatedly, "When I see somebody laughing, I feel like spitting in his face!"

"Don't think anybody will go on laughing. The war is drawing us in one step at a time. And once its flames have heated up, no one will be spared, whether he's on the front or at home."

And he wondered to himself again: What would the man say if he knew what went on in my fantastical abode? Curses. What do you all want? The end draws nigh. Life is precious and it makes sense to love it. As for you, Egypt, you're precious, too, but it doesn't make sense to love you! There must be a point in the upper reaches of space where differences melt away and destructive passions are wiped out.

By this time his peace of mind had been shattered entirely. He concluded that he was stupid and foolish. He thought to himself: Even so, I'm still not nearly stupid or foolish enough to be one of the greats of history. The torch of life, madness, and creative mystique . . . .

Ashmawi said, "It's only fair that tragedies should be distributed evenly."

"You're right."

"I don't understand!" said Abduh Badran.

Husni shot Amshawi a questioning look and he said, "For people who have troubles, when it rains, it pours."

"We're at the center of the world, so what do we expect?"

"Occupation, independence, 1956, Yemen, 1967, occupation!"

Concealing a growing feeling of irritation, he said, "Tomorrow a new homeland will be created."

"I'm not so sure about that," Abduh replied.

"That's because you've just come back from the hospital at a time when you'd been expecting to be getting ready for a wedding."

"Aahh, my country!"

"The land of the saints and the righteous!" Ashmawi chimed in. Then, with a vehemence that helped him recover some of his old ferocity, he cried, "O Arabs!"

Husni thought to himself for the third time: What life demands of us is so hard: weakness and strength, foolishness and wisdom, tenderness and roughness, ignorance and knowledge, ugliness and beauty, injustice and justice, slavery and freedom. And how am I ever to achieve all that? I've got neither ambition nor a position that's any good for getting things done. Nor have I got much life left to live. But I do love you, Egypt. So pardon me if you find that, along with my love for you, I also love life in its foolish hours of farewell!

20

The car pulled up in front of the Saqqara Nest Casino, and Hasan Hammouda and Mona Zahran got out together. They chose a lush, leafy spot on the south side of the garden, then sat down under a lamp that gave off a bluish light through the ivy. She was beautiful as usual, but a look of sorrow had settled deep in her eyes. Considering himself to have overcome the fundamental obstacles, he looked jovial with his tall stature, his deep, dark complexion, and the self-confident aura he exuded through his every gesture.

He looked at her for a long time, then began to smile as though he were inviting her to smile, too.

Breathing in deeply of the night air, which was redolent with the fragrance of greenery, he said, "This place is so quiet and peaceful, you'd think it belonged to another world."

"Yes," she whispered.

Then, feeling as though she'd admitted to more happiness than she had a right to, she added, "But we carry the burdens of the first world in our hearts."

"You've had your share of burdens and worries. But you're not the most unfortunate person on the face of the earth. Do you know what it means to lose four thousand hectares in a single second? Or to watch a father you've revered die of a heart attack? Or to see the reputation of a large, honorable family that's contributed to our national life since the Urabi Revolution be dragged through the mud?"

She hesitated for some time, then asked, "You know, don't you, that I'm no friend of feudalism?"

"That comes as no surprise to me, of course," he replied with a magnanimous smile. "After all, you're from the generation of the revolution. But perhaps you don't consider yourself an enemy of the student uprising?"

"That's different!"

"So be it. And now, back to your real worries. I tell you: None of what's happened is your fault in any way."

"But here we are, as you see. As for him . . . ."

"I repeat," he interrupted forcefully, "None of this is your fault."

Drawing his face near hers until the soft light reflected off the sides of his nose, he said, "Graves will go on filling up, and so will hospitals. But that won't stop us from eating, drinking, and getting married!"

She sighed audibly and murmured, "We were about to emigrate!"

Laughing, he replied, "I wanted badly to emigrate myself, but there was no hope of it. In any case, it would be better for us to find ourselves something else to talk about!"

Determined to stick to the point, she said, "People said, 'You're thinking of running away at a time when your country needs you most!'"

"Ah . . . I confess, I was brought up to be patriotic. But I don't care a whit anymore. Please, help me change the subject."

"Don't you care if our country wins?"

With a hopeless laugh he replied, "What I care about is for us to live peacefully and happily. If that's achieved through victory, then welcome to victory. And if it's achieved through defeat, then welcome to defeat."

She shot him a look of consternation.

"I don't understand," she said.

"I can't blame you. But I brought you here because I love you."

The fact is that he wanted to say more than this on the subject he'd been trying to avoid. He thought to himself: There's no getting away from politics. It's the very air we breathe.

"If they'd won the June war," he went on, "what would people like us have done? Defeat, as evil as it is, isn't without a blessing for those who suffered the defeat!"

Mona said nothing in reply, and he suspected that she hadn't grasped what he was saying. So, wanting to get his point across in a somewhat gentler fashion, he said, "One's country is the place where one finds happiness and an honorable life."

"And can we find happiness and an honorable life if we're defeated by Israel?"

To this he had no reply.

With a huff of exasperation, she said, "In any case, since you decided to emigrate once, I won't throw any stones at you."

The waiter came up unhurriedly and after the consultation with Mona, Hasan Hammouda ordered roast pigeon and a bottle of beer.

After the waiter had disappeared into the darkness of the garden, he said, "You've already thrown a thousand stones!"

Then, in a hortatory tone, he went on, "When troubles get worse, a person is entitled to do everything he can in search of happiness."

"That's a strange way of looking at things!"

"But it's only natural. And it's true. There's nothing like worry to rob happiness of its flavor!"

"I've got two dear friends," Mona said despondently, "whose plans for happiness were ruined on account of the war."

How will we ever break loose from this curse? He thought to himself. She then related the tragedies of Aliyat and Saniya while he feigned interest and concern.

He thought to himself: She's a hard nut to crack. But she'll be a wonderful wife. On the other hand, what do I want from her? It isn't that I hanker for fatherhood, stability, or immortality. All I want is love!

He raised his glass and said, "To our upcoming marriage!"

21

During the actors' visit to the front, Fitna Nadir didn't let Marzouq Anwar leave her side for a single minute. The journey began in the early morning, and it had been decided that they would go to Port Said, which was relatively calm by comparison with the explosive neighboring regions. The trip's organizers had chosen the Ras al-Barr route despite the fact that it was longer, since it was out of the range of enemy artillery fire. Consequently, everyone felt assured of a safe trip and pleasant companionship.

Fitna felt a secret disdain for her mentor, Ahmad Ridwan, who had stayed behind on the pretext of being ill when, in fact, his decision not to come was motivated by cowardice and his desire to play it safe at any cost.

They arrived in Port Said at midday and were invited straightaway to meet with the mayor. Words of welcome were heard from one side and from the other, words of concern and enthusiasm. Then a number of hours were spent visiting barracks in the city and some positions on the front. Hands met in warm greetings and looks were exchanged in admiration and goodwill. Regulars and officers alike gathered around their favorite actors and actresses, and Fitna thought of her lost brother, causing tears to well up in her eyes. Similarly, Marzouq thought of his friend Ibrahim Abduh, who lay in the hospital suspended between life and death. In the late afternoon they returned to Port Said, where they gathered in the mayor's public rest house.

Fitna suggested to Marzouq that the two of them go roaming a bit on the outskirts of the city. They strolled down a long, broad street that began from the square in front of the town hall. Within minutes, however, they were entirely cut off from the bustling life of the square with its cars, soldiers, and workers. Instead they found themselves in an all-encompassing void where they were engulfed by a frightening silence. There was no movement, no sound, and no shadow of man or beast. The buildings and houses stood along the sides of the street with their doors and windows shut as though no life had ever stirred within them. It was as if they were asleep, or dead, or skeletons, projects into which no life had yet been breathed. One's eyes longed for a glimpse of anything, and one's ears yearned to hear any sound: a window being flung open, a door creaking, clean laundry fluttering on a balcony, a young child shouting, a cat meowing, a dog barking. But no. There wasn't so much as a piece of paper blowing in the wind, a cigarette butt lying on the ground, or garbage piled along the curb. There was nothing, no sign of human life.

"It's a nightmare," Fitna whispered.

"The end of the world," Marzouq muttered.

"My heart—I don't know how to put into words what I'm feeling."

"A new experience, new feelings . . . ."

"It's as if I'm miserable, or really happy, like I'm dreaming of going back into my mother's womb."

"I feel free, completely free, of civilization and history."

"Is it possible for us to go out of our minds all of a sudden?"

"And maybe talk to departed spirits!"

They found themselves in front of a casino entrance. Its

doors were open, but no one was inside. A man who appeared to be its proprietor stood in the front part of the terrace. He was wearing a pullover and trousers, and had his sleeves rolled up. It was a startling, unexpected sight, and hard to believe.

"Maybe it's open on orders from the mayor."

"Maybe."

Fitna looked at the man, who greeted her with a smile of recognition.

"Might we drink a cup of coffee?" she asked him.

"Or anything else . . . ."

They sat down on the terrace as far out of sight of the empty street as they could. The coffee arrived, and they began sipping it with relish.

She said, "As happy as I was to be with the soldiers, I feel crazy here . . . ."

"The things they say really tug at your heartstrings, and it's obvious how anxious they are to fight."

"Yes. I can't imagine how people face death!"

"It's an atmosphere, a habit, and a dogma. And that's the problem."

"Behind it all is a sudden defeat that no one's been able to take in yet."

"Maybe they woke up crazy—like us!"

"To find everything like this deserted coffeeshop."

Looking pale, she went to the ladies' room, then came back with a smile on her face. When she returned, she found him taking deep drags on a cigarette.

He said, "I read today that deep inhalation of cigarette smoke is a major cause of lung cancer."

"Do you believe that?"

"I don't trust what I read in the newspapers anymore."

"Describe how you felt when your marriage plans fell through," she said playfully.

Pretending to be offended, he asked, "Are you making fun of people's misfortunes?"

"I'll admit," she said cheekily, "I was happy when I heard about it."

Blushing, he got up and said, "I'm going to the men's room."

He rushed off, and when he returned, he had washed his face and combed his hair.

"What did you do?" she asked, laughing.

"I cursed the times we live in!"

"But you're a star!"

"Art, like emigration, is an escape that's become the latest fashion."

"I don't like philosophy."

"I'm exempted from the draft," he said bitterly. "But why don't I volunteer with the freedom fighters?"

"So," she said mockingly, "the artist is a soldier, too."

With the same bitterness in his voice he replied, "The fact is, I've stopped believing in anything."

"But you want to get married!" she said.

"What do you expect when great expectations come to nothing?"

She whistled racily, then asked, "When do you think we'll be going back to Cairo?"

"At around dawn."

"I'm inviting you to a pre-dawn meal!"

Blushing again, he said, "You've already got two men. Isn't that enough for you?"

"One of them takes care of me, and the other is a mentor. But who is there to fill my empty heart in a city like this?"

As they got up to leave, he said, "I'm as good as married."

"Don't play hard to get," she said defiantly. "You're mine now. Haven't you realized that yet?"

22

Marzouq Anwar was standing in the garden outside the studio during a break when, unannounced and unexpected, he found his sister Saniya and his fiancée Aliyat standing before him. Flustered, he knew he was in a tight spot. Obliged to hold himself together, he muttered some words of welcome that were too muffled to be audible and reached out to shake their hands. For some time they were muted by the silence, and they were about to surrender to it indefinitely when it was broken by Saniya.

"You're not an easy person to find these days," she said edgily.

He had failed to appear at home for ten whole days, and he didn't know what to say. Saniya slipped her hand into Aliyat's purse and pulled out a letter.

"Is this from you?" she asked.

He bowed his head. He said nothing and made no objection.

"How incredibly shocking and regrettable."

Coming out of his silence, he muttered, "I share your sentiments."

"You're the one saying that?"

"Yes. I've been in torment for a long time. But an honorable life can't be based on a lie."

Her voice trembling, Aliyat asked, "So now you consider what we had to be a lie?"

"My esteem for you knows no bounds," he said gently, his voice tinged with sorrow. "I'm ashamed even to look at you. But this is the way things have to be."

"Does a great love die in a minute, only to be replaced by a new one?" Saniya asked bitterly.

"How despicable! You make me feel like a fool!" cried Aliyat.

"I'm sorry," he said. "There's nothing I can do about it. As for you, you're a beautiful young woman, and you've got a bright future ahead of you."

"Admit it: It's a whim, or a matter of convenience."

"That's not the way it is," he replied with a doleful shake of the head.

"I have to be going," said Aliyat with renewed agitation.

"Forgive me," he implored her.

Oblivious to being in a public place, she shouted, "I should thank my lucky stars that I've found out what you're really like!"

Her voice quavering as though she were about to cry, she moved away until she vanished into the darkness.

"How disgraceful!" Saniya said, her voice severe.

He shrugged his shoulders in resignation, then changed the subject, saying, "I've been so busy with work, I haven't had a chance to come home, but I'll visit you as soon as I can."

"The cost of being an actor is quite exorbitant, it seems!" she said sarcastically.

Ignoring her sarcasm, he replied, "I visited Ibrahim in the hospital, but it was hard for me to talk to him."

Looking down in distress, she said, "I guess you haven't heard that he's lost his sight."

Genuinely distraught, he stood there stunned for a few moments. Meanwhile, Saniya broke into loud sobs.

"Lost his sight?!"

"That's right."

"For good?"

"Of course."

"Is he aware of the situation?"

"Yes."

Silence reigned, allowing the sound of the breeze in the tree branches to make itself heard.

"I'm sorry to hear of your bad luck, Saniya."

"Well, it's better than Aliyat's!" she retorted.

"And what have you decided?"

"What a question! I'm going to hold on to him forever."

"Do you mean what you're saying?" he asked in amazement.

"Absolutely."

"He won't be neglected financially, but . . . ."

"I've thought it all over, and I've made my decision," she broke in.

After some hesitation, he said, "I hope your decision is based on sound thinking, and not on some passing emotional state."

"I know myself better than you think I do!"

"Well, then, my sincerest best wishes!"

Bringing the conversation back around to its original topic, she asked, "Isn't there any possibility of your going back on your decision about Aliyat?"

"Unfortunately not," he replied with calm determination.

"You're giving up a true love."

"We'll be marrying at the earliest opportunity."

Once again silence came between them until at last he said, "I admire you."

"Wish I could say the same," she retorted as she turned to leave.

23

Half-sitting and half-reclining on the middle divan under the chandelier, Husni Higgawi watched Ahmad Ridwan as he alternately paced back and forth and stood nervously with his elbow propped on the edge of the bar.

"Sit down, have a drink, and get hold of yourself," he said to him.

"I'll never find anybody that really understands me!" the director shouted furiously.

Husni thought to himself with a smile: Madness is the distinguishing mark of these years. He remembered having fallen in love once in his life, after which he'd forgotten all about it. Would he be destined to fall madly in love again as he stumbled into his sixth decade?

Ahmad Ridwan said angrily, "For a long time I noticed things but overlooked them. I thought they were just a passing fancy!"

"My dear Ahmad," Husni said soothingly, "allow me to remind you of that venerable companion known as Time!"

"I'm as strong as a mule."

"Sit down and have a drink."

"I'm seriously thinking of murdering her."

"Listen now to the former husband and the esteemed father!"

"Marriage and fatherhood don't preclude love or murder," he replied in disgust.

"If you'd only sit down and have a drink!"

Stamping his foot on the floor, he said, "We'd agreed to get married once. Do you realize what that means? It means she's losing me and Sheikh Yazid at the same time. Sheikh Yazid is the one who moved her from an old house on Saqlabi Street to an apartment in the Nile Building, and I'm the one who created her!"

"We might be able to create, but it may not be easy to control our creations forever."

"She's a madwoman, and the daughter of a madwoman. Doesn't she realize that her light will go out, and that he won't be able to find anyone to sign a contract with?"

"Take a trip to Europe."

"To hell with the trip, and to hell with Europe!"

"I'm sad for you, old partner."

"Is that the best medicine you've got to offer?"

"I know of a similar tragedy. After all, I know Marzouq's former fiancée, and she's suffering just the way you are."

"She'll get over him in a half-hour or so."

Laughing in spite of himself, Husni said, "So, you're the only real lover in the whole country!"

Ahmad said with a groan, "May God burn her up the way she's burning me up. The fact is, I can't imagine life without her."

"Be patient. She's unpredictable, and I bet you this marriage won't last more than a month!"

"And all I have to do is be patient and suffer!"

"Sit down and have a drink."

"All you've got to offer are platitudes."

"What can I do?"

"As for me, I can murder."

"No. You're not the bloodthirsty type."

With the rage of someone haunted by humiliating memories, he said, "I even proposed marriage to her!"

"God be with you!"

"And what did the little whore do? She decided to get married all right, but to somebody else!"

He clenched his fist menacingly and continued, "They're making preparations to deal with possible air raids, and they're expecting all-out war. Great. I predict that a catastrophe is going to strike this damned country."

Husni thought about the blue color they painted the windows and lamps, and the red brick barricades they put in front of the doors. Recoiling at the thought, he said to himself: My only consolation in life is my lavish, much-frequented abode. So how would life go on if it were destroyed? How would life go on if I found myself displaced and living in a tent?

He said to Ahmad, "I'd advise you to take a trip abroad after you've finished shooting your film."

Turning with a groan toward the bar to fill a glass, Ahmad said bitterly, "I need a really long trip."

24

The telephone rang on Mona Zahran's desk. It was Salim Ali. With the utmost earnestness and respect, he asked her to meet him "for a few minutes" at Dar al-Shay al-Hindi or anywhere else she might prefer. She declined on principle, but he pressed her. She asked why he wanted to see her, and he replied that he couldn't go into the details over the telephone, but that he had something to say that was of the greatest importance.

Anxious and distraught, Mona went to see him at the time they had agreed on. When they met, they shook hands and sat down together. She noticed from the time she first set eyes on him that he wasn't well, which pleased her. However, she wasn't pleased by the fact that she felt pleased. He had lost a significant amount of weight, the light in his eyes had grown dull, and he looked ashen. In his eyes she could see a reflection of her own image, and it seemed to her that he, too, had noticed a change that arrested his attention. Had sorrow tinged her with its dark hues without her realizing it? He thanked her for "being so kind as to come," and she in turn told him candidly that she didn't want to stay any longer than necessary. Her reply discomfited him somewhat, although he'd been expecting it.

"Since the last time we met, both of us have been through tough experiences, and I wish I could have been there for you in your ordeal."

She made no comment.

He went on, "Throughout this entire time I've acted like a fool."

She still said nothing.

He continued, saying, "I got married as though marriage were a form of suicide."

Although she regretted it as soon as she'd opened her mouth, she replied, "I didn't manage to congratulate you at the time!"

He swallowed the jibe as though he hadn't heard it.

"And I hear you'll be getting married soon?"

"Very soon," she replied.

Filled with such overwhelming emotions that he feared he wouldn't be able to keep them under control, he remained silent for a while so as to collect his scattered thoughts.

Then he said, "Pardon me, but I'd like to ask you: Are you getting married for true love?"

"What right do you have to ask me such a question?" she protested.

"I have no right at all to ask it. However, I've learned from experience that any rash decision we make impacts our lives for the worse and usually leads to disaster."

"Preaching doesn't become you in the least!"

Heaving a deep sigh, he confessed, "Mona, I love you. I still love you the way I did in the very beginning. I can't live without you."

She shot him a look of fury and disdain.

"What have I done to myself?" he went on. "I married a cheap dancer. Why? Frankly, it was because of you."

"Because of me?"

"You didn't give our love the respect it deserved. I wronged it myself with my pigheadedness, and you wounded it with your pride. That's how some people undermine their true happiness!"

Furrowing her brow in the hope of looking so severe that her feelings wouldn't show, she said, "What's the use of digging up things that are dead and buried?"

"They shouldn't die."

"But they *have* died, and that's that!"

"I don't believe death has any power over them."

"That's your illusion, and yours alone!"

"My life was nothing but misery until I liberated myself by getting a divorce."

She looked into the distance as though something had caught her attention, and made no comment.

"My marriage turned out to be nothing but a silly game, and I realized that I couldn't go on living with the poor woman. There was no love to hold us together, and we had nothing in common. What can I say? She's an unlucky woman. She's been corrupted by night-life, which has dried up the springs of humanity in her heart. Her life has turned into nothing but an unbroken chain of infernal habits and a deadly addiction to opium!"

"I don't know why you're talking to me about this."

"Because I love you."

He paused for a minute to let his words sink in. Then he continued, "If love means anything to you, you've got to listen to me. And I know that you hold love to be sacred. If you love this other man, then I apologize for wasting your time. If, on the other hand, you're hoping to fill an emptiness through marriage, then remember that the emptiness that comes from the need for love can be filled by nothing but love itself."

"What do you want?" she asked testily.

"For us to go back to the love we had."

She laughed indifferently and said, "What a ridiculous thing to ask for!"

"It's the only thing I'm asking for in life."

Determined to keep her emotions in check, she shrugged her shoulders nonchalantly and said nothing.

"Hope is what keeps me going."

Rising to leave, she said, "I have to go now."

He followed her out, saying, "I won't give up hope. Goodbye. And my heart will be with you forever."

25

Ibrahim sat on the couch flanked by his fiancée Saniya and his sister Aliyat. He was clad in a loose-fitting tunic, and from the neckband emerged his shorn head, his thin, pallid face, and the dark glasses that concealed his eyes. It was his first day home from the hospital and he had received an outpouring of consoling, encouraging words. And now no one was left in the room but the three of them. He leaned his head against the cool wall and began working to gain mastery over his will. For him, combat was over, a history had drawn to a close, and light had vanished forever. When the reality of things had first descended upon him, he'd said, "I wish I'd died." But he wasn't saying that anymore. Instead, an extraordinary warmth flowed into his heart now that he was home. He no longer doubted that life was better than death.

Meanwhile, Saniya chattered nonstop. She said with a laugh, "'As long as there's life, there's hope.' I don't know how many times I've written it or said it. Unfortunately, I've forgotten who coined the expression, but I never really understood what it meant until now."

He smiled at the sound of her beloved voice.

"I'll read to you," she went on, "and you'll learn to read Braille. You'll forge a new path for yourself!"

"Saniya," he murmured, "I'm so grateful. You're an angel."

He hesitated a bit, then went on, "But I release you from any commitment you may have made before!"

Placing her forefinger affectionately over his lips, she replied, "I didn't hear a thing."

"But really, think about it carefully. Our most misguided decisions are the ones we make when we're overly emotional."

"I *have* thought about it," she countered resolutely, "and it's become clear to me that I don't need to think at all."

"I don't want to be selfish."

"It's *my* decision," she reminded him. "Besides, how can you describe yourself as selfish after having sacrificed something so precious?"

Resting his head on his hand, he said, "But I'm embarrassed."

"As for me, I'm quite content."

"Believe her," Aliyat said to him. "I know her inside and out."

Outside, storm winds raged. Then rain poured down for five minutes, after which the sky cleared, and warmth, purity, and the sweet fragrance of the heavens diffused through the atmosphere.

Ibrahim went to bed and before long had fallen into a deep slumber. Aliyat and Saniya sat alone in the sitting room with a pot of tea and a bowl full of green fava beans before them. Saniya seemed happy, bursting with emotions she had yet to express. Her heart welled up with inspiration that gave her a sense of boldness, courage, and readiness for self-sacrifice.

She said, "I've been thinking . . . ."

Aliyat shot her a questioning look.

"I don't want to deceive him!"

"No!" Aliyat said in alarm.

"I don't want . . . ."

"Although he's young, my brother has absorbed my parents' views on this sort of thing in particular," Aliyat interrupted fearfully, "and he wouldn't understand you at all."

"I think he would."

"No. It's enough that you're so completely devoted to him."

"But doesn't he have the right to know?" insisted Saniya skeptically.

"No. I don't acknowledge any right that will bring nothing but misery. And he wouldn't understand you!"

"And if it occurs to him to ask?"

"It's enough that you're devoted to him. And devotion wipes out what went before it."

Worried, the two of them sat thinking in silence until Aliyat said, "We didn't let our hearts be broken by pleasure, so we shouldn't let them be broken by true love."

Saniya sensed from Aliyat's tone of voice that she was bewailing her own misfortune. Moved by her friend's pain, she said, "You'll find love again. It's always a part of life!"

"Peace brings as many tragedies as war does."

"I think a tragedy has befallen my brother Marzouq without his realizing it."

Aliyat nodded despondently. Then, responding to a memory that had suddenly come back to her, she said, "And Dr. Ali Zahran is a victim of absurdity."

As Saniya remembered Mona Zahran, a smile passed across her lips.

When Aliyat asked her what had made her smile, she said, "Mona Zahran and her decisions!"

Laughing, Aliyat said, "She should publish a daily report on the most recent state of her heart."

"Do you think she's broken up with Hasan Hammouda for good?"

"I think she'll marry Salim Ali at the earliest opportunity."

"Despite her craziness, it's a wise decision."

"They're both crazy."

They both fell silent for a while. Then Aliyat asked, "When are they getting married?"

"Mona and Salim?"

"No, Marzouq and Fitna!"

"I don't know," replied Saniya gloomily. "I hear they're going to get married after they finish shooting the film."

And with that, Saniya felt a despondency that soon dried up the springs of her inspiration.

26

Hasan Hammouda had been invited to dinner at the villa of a journalist by the name of Safwat Morgan on Ahmad Shawqi Street. The party gathered on the veranda overlooking the garden, and Hasan Hammouda sat between his two friends, Safwat and his wife, Nihad al-Rahmani. He ate heartily and drank copiously, all the while determined to put on an air of indifference as though the crisis had passed.

Safwat Morgan said to him, "I was afraid I'd find you miserable."

With an ease that suggested candor he replied, "There's no need to be miserable!"

Then he added, "It's a matter of dignity, that's all."

The fact was, he'd never imagined he would find himself in the situation Mona had created for him. He'd been in the process of setting the wedding date, with plans to host the celebration at the Auberge Hotel, and word had gotten around to family, friends, and colleagues. So when, with her customary boldness, she had faced him with her decision not to go through with it, he'd been dumbfounded. He'd been dumbfounded and bewildered, and he had begged her to reconsider. He had fallen in love with her, was filled with admiration for her, and had dreamed of a happy life with her. Damn it all! Was he destined to suffer in love the way he'd suffered in politics?

Nihad al-Rahmani asked him, "So what do you intend to do now, dear?"

Gravely he replied, "I'll take to the mountains like the criminals in my native Upper Egypt and work as a highway robber."

Safwat laughed.

"What do you want with today's girls, anyway?" he asked playfully. "Thank God things turned out the way they did!"

To which Nihad added, "The best thing for you to do now is to find yourself a sensible marriage partner before you miss the boat."

"What do you mean by 'sensible?'" he queried resentfully.

"I mean someone who's nearer your age, and who comes from a family similar to yours."

"It seems you've got a bride lined up!" Safwat said to her.

"There's always a good bride somewhere around. What, does that surprise you?"

"Hold off on me until I've gotten through the transition phase."

Then he thought to himself cynically: The law of things dictates that Safwat the socialist should marry someone like Nihad from a high-class family. As for me, I have to marry a plebeian!

Safwat said, "What happened between you and Mona is a rerun of an old story that happened twenty years ago."

Hasan Hammouda was speechless for a few seconds, then laughed.

"What story?" asked Nihad.

Safwat replied, "It's an old story in which Hasan was the hero!"

"I wasn't the hero, I was the villain," Hasan corrected him with a sardonic laugh.

"What was her name? I've completely forgotten."

"Samra Wagdi," said Hasan.

"I've never heard her name or her story," said Nihad.

"We were law students, and our friend fell passionately in love with her. She was from a big family, although her particular branch didn't own anything."

"And he asked for her hand?" asked Nihad.

"No, he just fell passionately in love with her. And he was an audacious lover. He would sneak in to meet her at night in her uncle's mansion on the Nile while everybody else was asleep."

"*The Arabian Nights*! My goodness!"

"One night the guard caught wind of him. He ran after him. He fired. The bullet hit the girl in the cheek and our friend ran away. During the investigation, the girl said she'd heard someone walking around outside and that she'd come out to call the guard, and that that was how the bullet had hit her!"

"Wonderful!"

"But her face was disfigured, or at least, her cheek."

"Poor thing!"

"And just as our friend fled from the mansion, he fled from her life."

"From her life?!"

"And for good."

Nihad started to comment, but then thought better of it. Hasan noticed it and said with a chuckle, "Go ahead, pronounce the verdict. I've already heard everything there is to say."

"You should have held on to her!"

"It was amusement, not love, and I was young and crazy. And now here I am getting the same treatment!"

"What happened to her after that?" Safwat Morgan asked him.

"She owns a ladies' apparel and accessories shop on Sherif Street," Hasan replied.

"Have you ever run into each other by chance?"

"Once at the Pigalle Bar, and she ignored me completely."

"You're not the cruel type as far as I know," said Nihad.

"The fact is, I suffered my share of pain over it. Then when the blessed revolution came along and I faced one tragedy after another, it purged me of the pain through things that were even more terrible."

"You have a rare opportunity before you now. Marry her!"

He guffawed and said, "A splendid ending to a melodrama. As for the reality, she's now a notorious pimp!"

"A pimp?!"

"An amateur pimp."

"What do you mean?" Safwat asked.

"Her house is a meeting place for girls, and she has legendary control over them. She spends evenings with them in friends' houses, not for money, but just for the entertainment!"

"What a denouement!"

"I've heard that she says sarcastically that the age of innocence has come to an end along with reactionism, feudalism, and colonialism."

Nihad asked him, "Don't you consider yourself responsible for the way she's ended up?

"Not at all, my dear. She could just as well have ended up as a wife, an irresponsible shop owner, or a saint for that matter."

He thought to himself: Why do they engage in this sentimental stock-taking for the sake of a dead past, and forget my suffering and my wounded dignity? Isn't Samra Wagdi a thousand times happier than I am? Didn't our family lose a nephew in the raids that were launched inside our territory? Not to mention my father's death and the way our family's reputation was unjustly besmirched. Even so, the most dangerous thing is for a forty-year-old man to let himself be ruined by a failed love affair.

Turning to Safwat, he asked, "What about the news?"

Safwat, a man whose opinion was always held in high esteem, replied, "There's nothing new. But I think things are getting better."

"Shame on you," said Hasan Hammouda irritably.

Safwat laughed a belly laugh and said, "I'd forgotten I was talking to a man whose heart is with the Israeli army against the Egyptians!"

Not without a feeling of indignation, Hasan asked, "So is that how you perceive my position?"

"The issue first and foremost is one of a patriotic attitude."

"What patriotic attitude! As for democracy or socialism, the United States or Russia . . . if you have the right to love Russia, don't we have the right to love the United States?"

Safwat replied seriously, "The important thing is what the people want."

"What people?"

"The people. The ordinary folks that you don't know."

He felt himself seething with mockery and bitterness, hatred and resentment. At that moment he loathed everything, even the garden redolent with the fragrance of orange blossoms, the sultry night, Safwat Morgan, and Nihad al-Rahmani.

Be patient, he said to himself. After all, in the twinkling of an eye unforeseen calamity might strike.

27

Aliyat attended two weddings in a single week: a humble affair that brought together her blind brother and Saniya, and a celebration held in the Umar al-Khayyam Hall that joined Mona Zahran and Salim Ali. She thought to herself: Whatever friendship I might have had with Saniya and Mona, it won't stay the same now that they're married.

She'd learned as much from previous experiences, and she felt a horrible emptiness the likes of which she had never felt in her entire life. At the same time, she detested the idea of going back to a life of diversion and frivolous play, since the fact was that she longed for love.

In the evening she went to visit Husni Higgawi in response to an invitation she had received from him by telephone while she was at the ministry. Receiving her warmly, he kissed her on her cheeks and said, "I'd expected you to visit me a long time ago."

When she made no reply, he said, "What are you doing these days?"

"I'm eating, drinking, and sleeping," she replied apathetically.

"We have to learn from the bitterness of the trials we go through not to grieve too much, no matter how bad things are!"

In the same apathetic tone she replied, "I'm learning. But as you know, education takes time."

"You're brave, and I'm confident of your future."

She laughed in spite of herself, and he cast her an inquisitive look.

"What made you laugh?" he asked.

"How handsome you are in a preacher's robe!"

He went over to the bar to fill two glasses with his famous cocktail.

"Why did you invite me? Have you got a new film in mind?"

He presented her with the glass and said, "I don't forget my girls the way they forget me, and I think about their futures. Consequently, I've spoken to the director Ahmad Ridwan about you!"

"About me?" she murmured, her eyes suddenly aflame with interest and astonishment.

"I told him you were a wonderful, beautiful girl and that you'd be good screen material."

"Me?" she cried in amazement.

"You, of course."

She laughed nervously and said, "I can't imagine. I don't . . . "

"Did Marzouq Anwar imagine or think he could?"

"I'm not an actress. And have you forgotten about my father?"

"He'll blow his top, of course, and he'll reject the idea. But I'll have a long talk with him, and in the end he'll give in!"

"He's more hard-nosed than you imagine. But he isn't the real problem. The problem is here . . . ."

She pointed to herself.

"Let's leave that to events."

"So, you're serious then?"

"And he's prepared to test you!"

"Why are you thinking about this, anyway?" she asked.

"So that your life won't be nothing but eating, drinking, and sleeping!" he replied with a laugh.

She concealed her nervousness with a laugh, and he said, "I expected you to be more enthusiastic than this. After all, life requires us to be enthusiastic even in the worst of circumstances."

The two of them drank together, and she closed her eyes to think while he went pacing back and forth between the bar and the television.

She opened her eyes, they met his, and he asked her, "What do you say?"

"So be it. It can't be any worse than anything that's already happened."

He laughed and said, "Affliction is the mother of wisdom."

"The streets are nearly blacked out!"

"You can't understand anything or conclude anything . . . ."

"Where the future's concerned, anything is possible."

"In circumstances like these, it's best to treasure every minute that's free of disaster."

"People are saying all sorts of things."

"If Cairo were hit, it would be the end of the world."

"My poor brother. May God take him by the hand."

With an air of seriousness Husni Higgawi said, "My older brother's son was called in for the draft yesterday. As for my sister, who's a wealthy widow, she did the impossible to spare her oldest son the draft. She sent him to Canada as an emigrant."

"How did she manage that?"

He let out a short laugh and said, "Use your imagination! In any case, he was killed last week in a crash!"

She let escape a gasp of shocked amazement.

"Laugh if you like!" said Husni.

"Do we lack a fighting spirit?" she asked.

"Visitors to the front report finding high morale. But their families are living in confusion!"

Then, in a tone of certainty, he continued, "And don't forget the freedom fighters. They're the miracle of this phase!"

The doorbell rang and, looking expectant, he went to open it, saying, "It's probably Ahmad Ridwan. So be brave, please!"

28

Fitna Nadir was present for the final day of filming on her own, since Marzouq had no role in the last scene. The work was finished at around 9:30 p.m. Congratulations were exchanged, glasses of fruit juice were served, and Ahmad Ridwan distributed money to the filming crew. He invited Fitna for a cup of coffee at the buffet, so she changed her clothes and followed him there. As they sat together drinking tea and eating cookies, she wondered to herself: Is this our farewell rendezvous? Reports had reached her to the effect that he was preparing to introduce a new actress to the scene, with the intention of doing away with her. She didn't care much, though, since she was confident of the success she'd achieved among the masses. At the same time, she preferred to avoid a silly, meaningless quarrel. She hoped he would come to his senses if such was possible.

After eyeing her at length, he asked, "What are you thinking about?"

"How we can stay friends," she replied with candor.

"Friendship is no substitute for love," he replied sourly.

"You should judge me fairly," she said.

"Does that mean you're really getting married?"

"I told you so at the time when I made the decision."

"But I wasn't just something peripheral in your life!" he protested.

"There's no question of that," she admitted. "You're the one that made my success possible!"

"I thank you," he said hopefully, "but why marriage, Fitna? There's no reason to get married!"

"It seems you don't believe me yet."

"It's hard for me to believe you."

"Don't you believe in the possibility of madness?"

"Since I'm mad myself," he said in resignation, "I do believe in madness, but . . . ."

"But?" she encouraged him to go on.

"But can somebody be so mad that he makes light of the future?"

Here he was resorting to threats again! So he hadn't changed after all.

"The future is in God's hands alone," she said.

"I'm impressed by your faith!" he said sarcastically.

She didn't laugh.

"So, then," he said, drawing his face near hers, "let our relationship stay the way it was."

Indignant, she said, "But I'm serious, sir!"

"So then," he said furiously, "you weren't serious before?"

She sighed but made no reply.

"Damn!" he muttered, his voice full of fury and bitterness.

Then he added menacingly, "I'm afraid the flame might go out for both of us!"

"If we truly intend to succeed, we won't have to face such a fate."

"I don't think you understand yourself. The only thing you love is acting!"

"Leave me to my fate," she begged him.

"You're driving me into an abyss!" he cried, his face contorted with rage.

"I have unbounded faith in your good judgment."

"It's disgraceful for you to admit that the feelings you had before were a sham!"

"Let's not talk about the past," she said, furrowing her brow in exasperation.

Then, placing her hand on his, she said, "Open your heart to a new friendship."

"Don't talk about love as though you don't know anything about it," he said irately.

In muted desperation she muttered, "It's no use."

"It's no use!" he repeated nastily.

They both fell silent, and she asked herself: How will this unbearable session end? She was called to the telephone, and she got up with a sigh of relief. As for him, he began watching her from a distance as she spoke.

He saw her hang up the receiver in haste and confusion. Something had happened. Something serious. Unimaginably serious. Looking this way and that as though she'd lost her senses, she started to leave, forgetting all about her purse. He picked up the purse and began running toward her, but no sooner had he uttered her name than she screamed in his face, "You . . . you . . . you're the criminal!"

And she made a frenzied dash for her car.

29

Red-eyed, Fitna collapsed onto the metal chair. Marzouq lay in his hospital bed, his head and face wrapped in bandages. Right after the accident he had undergone a complex operation on his lower jaw, chin, and forehead. In the adjacent waiting room sat Ibrahim, Saniya, and Aliyat. Even Ahmad Ridwan came to visit him. However, when he found the atmosphere hostile, he beat a quick retreat.

When, after a suitable period of time had passed, Marzouq was questioned in the investigation, he said he had been walking down Ibn Ayyub Street in the early evening. The street had been empty and it had been completely dark. Then suddenly he had been assaulted by one or more persons who had beaten him in the face until he lost consciousness, and when he came to, he was in the hospital. He was asked the standard questions on whether he had enemies or whether he had leveled accusations at anyone, and he replied in the negative. However, the investigation led him to mention his love affair and the circumstances surrounding it, which led in turn to the interrogation of Ahmad Ridwan and even Aliyat Abduh. Sheikh Yazid wasn't in Egypt at the time, and Ahmad Ridwan denied any connection to the incident, as did Aliyat. Therefore the investigations continued in an atmosphere shrouded in mystery.

For his family and others who loved him, concern focused around an important question.

"I wonder how much his face will change?" Saniya said.

"His future depends on it," replied Ibrahim.

"Fitna cried hard," she said.

"She was crying both for him and for herself."

The waiting period weighed heavily on loving hearts. And then Marzouq left the hospital with a new look. Despite the miracles made possible by modern medicine, he came out with a different face. It wasn't ugly. But it had lost its personality, its flavor, its spirit. There was a small depression on one side of his forehead and a crookedness in the jaw that lent his face an uncharacteristic harshness. In addition, his chin sloped back in a way it hadn't before. When he saw his image in the mirror, he looked at it for a long time in dismay until his eyes clouded over. Then he doubled over in despair and cried, "I'm done for!"

The picture of disappointment, he turned to Fitna and said again, "I'm done for, Fitna!"

"No!" she said fervently as she wrapped her arms around his neck.

"I'm done for, and you know it."

"No!"

"No?!"

"Maybe . . . maybe . . . ."

"Maybe?" he interrupted her questioningly.

Lowering her eyes, she said, "There will be a number of successful roles for a capable actor like you."

"So indirectly, you're saying you agree with me," he cried hopelessly.

Holding him close, she said, "Let's not think about that now."

"Is there anything more important to think about?"

With a playful pinch on the cheek, she said, "We're getting ready for the wedding!"

He gazed at her absently, his left eye twitching and narrowing.

"What?" he asked.

"The wedding, my dear ingrate!"

"Is this just pigheadedness on your part?"

"No!" she shouted angrily.

And he thought to himself: Does she really mean what she's saying? Do such miracles really happen on earth?

As for her, her heart was bursting with love, compassion, and defiance. She was determined to shatter the rigid armor of shame and to spit in the faces of those who gloat over others' misfortune.

Holding him tightly to her bosom she said, "Let's get ready for the wedding!"

30

Husni Higgawi took her into his arms and she lay her head trustingly on his chest, making him aware of how badly she longed for affection. Patting her on the back, he said, "The cares of this world and the next are etched on your sweet face, Aliyat."

Loosing herself from his embrace, she plopped down in the armchair and asked him, "Where have you been lately?"

"I went to Yugoslavia to take part in a short film festival," he replied.

"Haven't you heard what happened to Marzouq Anwar?"

"It's the talk of the town in artistic circles, and many people suspect Ahmad Ridwan of being behind it. However, it's just speculation, and there's no evidence to back it up. What do you think?"

"I don't know. I myself was questioned during the investigation!"

"I would have done anything to spare you that, dear."

"And Fitna and Marzouq are married now."

"That's the talk of the town, too. But nobody can predict what will come of it!"

"Saniya and Ibrahim are happy," she said languidly, "and theirs is a similar situation."

"No, it isn't. There's a fundamental difference. But you haven't told me what happened with you."

"What do you mean?"

"I mean with the accused Ahmad Ridwan."

"I failed miserably," she replied casually. "I don't have an actress's bone in my body."

He looked at her pityingly and said, "Is that what's making you sad?"

"No."

"But you missed me when I was gone. Why's that?"

"I came knocking on your door every evening."

With a sardonic smile he said, "So, did you finally realize that I'm the one you're really in love with?"

Without saying a word, she pointed to her abdomen.

Then she said, "There's something here I don't want."

"No!" he cried in disbelief.

"It's the truth."

"But you're always so careful!"

"I'm tired of being careful," she said bitterly, "the way I'm tired of life."

He gazed at her, recalling the sight of the Adriatic Islands as they appear from Dubrovnik on a moonlit night.

Then he asked her, "Whose is it?"

"You'll never guess!"

"U Thant?"

"An anonymous tourist with a blond beard and braided hair who invited me to dinner one night!"

Husni let out a long laugh, then said, "Keep it. It'll be a precious little pearl!"

"I nearly lost my mind while you were gone."

"You've let sadness get the better of you more than you ought to," he said caringly.

Speaking with a powerful emotion that augured a storm of tears, she said, "First there was the investigation, then their wedding, and I felt as though the whole world had died and would never come back to life."

Feeling cheerless, he filled a couple of glasses and presented her with hers, saying, "To your health."

They emptied their glasses at the same time.

Then he said—not truthfully, but out of genuine compassion, "While I was sitting in an underground garden in Dubrovnik, I thought of you, and I felt an extraordinary longing for you!"

"Maybe I was thinking about you as I rang your doorbell and found nobody home."

"My heart is with you. Don't worry, dear."

She heaved a loud sigh that reverberated like a musical note in the room's magical atmosphere.

He was laboring to master a desire that had sprung up suddenly in his pores, an unexpected, tender desire to make love to her. However, he didn't let on. Instead, he went to the telephone and dialed a number.

"Hello, Samra? How are you? It's nice that you recognized my voice. I need you for something urgent. Right now if possible. Goodbye."

As he came back to join her he said, "Do you know Samra Wagdi?"

She shook her head.

"Well, it's time you got to know her."

31

Hasan Hammouda had gone forty years without giving marriage so much as a thought until he met Mona Zahran. But after his plans to marry her fell through, marriage was all he could think about. One evening Hasan Hammouda invited Madam Nihad and her husband Safwat Morgan for dinner at his mansion on al-Fadl Street in Agouza. It was an enormous mansion with a large garden that he'd inherited from his mother, and he lived there alone with the servants. He enjoyed the distinction of having a top-notch chef who could easily have been the pride and joy of a first-class restaurant. Hasan Hammouda was a big eater and a connoisseur of good food, both of them traits he shared with Madam Nihad. Safwat, on the other hand, contented himself with a couple of glasses of whiskey and a bit of broiled meat, vegetables, and fruit. The conversation revolved around marriage, and it was Hasan himself who had brought up the subject despite his well-known passion for endless political discussions.

"I want to hear the latest news on your bride!" he said to Madam Nihad.

"I bet you'll be married before the year's out," said Safwat.

Madam Nihad replied, "She's a widow with an only daughter in university. And like you, she's from a large family."

Unimpressed, he said, "That means she has to be at least forty years old."

"She's forty years old exactly!"

"But I'm forty myself, and I need a young wife!" he protested.

"I'm not a matchmaker!" said Nihad, laughing. "You'll just have to find one on your own: at the cinema, at a nightclub, or on the street!"

"I've got no time to go looking," he said hopelessly, "and if it weren't for a criminal case I was invited to defend, I wouldn't have met Mona Zahran."

"All you have to do is wait for another case to come along, then," said Nihad.

"Besides, is a younger woman really right for you?" Safwat asked him.

"Why wouldn't she be?"

"Women of the younger generation have a new perspective on life and love."

Hasan replied without hesitation, "In this area, I'm more progressive than you think!"

"You're not the first person to be a reactionary in politics and a progressive in love!" Safwat said with a chuckle.

Hasan Hammouda's dark-skinned face clouded over with rage and his eyes glinted more sharply than usual. It always infuriated him to be accused of being a reactionary. He considered democracy to be the pinnacle of progress, and everything else to be some sort of Nazism or fascism. As he understood it, democracy was an approach to dealings among members of a society's elite, the elite being the people who control society's real interests, cultured people, the intelligentsia. As for ordinary folks, he didn't recognize them or even include them in the category of "humanity." Consequently, he hadn't deferred to the tremendous populist wave that had been unleashed by the revolution, and he mocked those of his own class who had been so moved by it that they began shaking their family trees in the hope of coming across some poor, working-class branch to which they could cling for refuge in the midst of the violent storm that was pulling them up by their roots. He had always taken pride in his upper-class origins and in the giants among his paternal uncles and ancestors, and he took an aristocratic, bigoted view of things and people. Having been rescued from the discussion of marriage by Safwat Morgan's passing comment, he was brought back to the topic that had always been dearest to his heart, namely, politics.

"American democracy, reactionary?! The United States is a scientific nation, and through science it's risen above communism's cock and bull stories and false prophecies!"

"We never stop talking. No one can out-talk us. Meanwhile, we're attacked on our very own soil."

Exasperated, Hasan Hammouda said, "The problem is that we're a defeated nation that refuses to admit that it's been defeated!"

Looking over at Safwat, he asked, "When do you think we'll acknowledge reality?"

Safwat replied as he lit a cigarette, "The Russians are going to be taking an important new step in strengthening our defenses."

The Russians, too! He hated the Russians' guts. If it hadn't been for them, June 5 would have been the day of true happiness and paradise restored.

He asked him, "Will we be able to hold out until the new Russian supplies arrive?"

"They won't let us be defeated again!" he replied confidently.

"Congratulations on this enviable safety!"

Safwat laughed and said, "The Russians aren't exploitative."

Considering it a joke, Hasan Hammouda guffawed. Through laughter he vented his smoldering bitterness and hatred, and gave voice to his gruesome unspoken dreams.

Nihad, who wearied quickly of politics, asked him merrily, "If you want to get married, why don't you put an ad in the newspaper?"

Hasan chuckled and so did Safwat, who seconded the idea, saying, "I suggest the following: H.H., successful lawyer, wealthy, from an aristocratic family, forty years old, with American leanings and an Israeli worldview, wishes to marry a beautiful, modern, sophisticated twenty-year-old girl."

Still chuckling, Hasan said, "I'll get a reply from the Minister of the Interior!"

32

Marzouq and Fitna spent their honeymoon in Aswan, and when they returned to Cairo, they set up household in an apartment on Finney Street and prepared to face the unknown. Marzouq had recovered a good deal of his lost confidence and had begun to dream of a brighter future than he'd heretofore allowed himself to. Fitna was invited to play a leading role in a film, so she suggested that Marzouq play the male lead. However, her suggestion was rejected in a manner she considered unacceptable, so she haughtily turned down the offer. The same scenario was repeated later that same week. At that point,

Marzouq considered that the issue called for a discussion. His confidence shaken and his dreams evaporating, he broached the subject with a heavy heart and forlorn determination.

He said to her, "You can't turn down any more offers. Otherwise . . . ."

"I'm convinced that you'd add an element of success to any film," she interrupted.

"What matters is for other people to be convinced of the same thing. So, make suggestions if you'd like, but don't reject what's offered you."

He felt as though the success he'd once achieved belonged to some other person, and he said to her sorrowfully, "It would be best for me to think seriously about the government position I never filled."

"You mean, work six hours for seventeen pounds!" she asked in horror.

"I've got to adjust to reality, no matter how bitter it is."

Refusing to undertake childish adventures or give in to crazy whims, he said, "It's obvious that I'm no longer fit for leading roles."

"There's more than one leading role in every film," she said gently. "But beware of taking secondary roles. They're a trap you'll never get out of."

Indeed, they were a trap. Their elegant residence was a trap, too, as was the love for the sake of which he'd sacrificed his humanity. Life had turned its back on him to the point where he felt loathsome.

The telephone rang. It was Ahmad Ridwan, wanting to know if it would be all right for him to pay them a visit. Fitna looked over at Marzouq as if to ask him what he thought, and in spite of the agitation he felt, he said, "If it's work-related, let him come."

Ahmad Ridwan came at the agreed-upon time. When he came in, he bowed respectfully in greeting, at the same time avoiding the risk of a handshake. He sat down politely, with an air of neither gloating nor conceit.

He said, "There's a cloud of suspicion hanging over me."

He cast his eyes back and forth between the two of them, then continued, "And we need to dispel it, since there's no justification for it, and because we have no choice but to work together."

He heard no comment. He could feel their glances stinging his face like live embers.

Again he went on, "It was ridiculous for me to be called in for interrogation. It hurt me deeply, as it ought to hurt someone who's innocent in every sense of the word."

When he still received no reply, he turned to Marzouq and said, "I'm not a criminal. I'm an artist like you, and my love for my coworkers is legendary."

Realizing that she hadn't welcomed him or offered him anything, Fitna gestured toward the bar, saying, "Sorry. Won't you have something to drink?"

He got up and went to the bar, then took the bottle of Courvoisier, his favorite drink, and filled a glass. Then he came back and carried on with what he'd been saying to Marzouq.

"There's more than one person who might be suspected of committing the crime. It didn't give me any satisfaction to be declared innocent. What really matters to me is for *you* to be convinced of my innocence."

All he heard in reply was the sound of breathing, and his features registered a look of disappointment.

"Open your heart to me," he said, "and tell me what you're thinking."

He fixed his gaze on Marzouq until the latter said, "I don't think about it anymore, and I'm leaving the mysteries to the police."

"Wonderful. Let's wait, then. I'm fully confident that the guilty party will be found. And now, let's talk business!"

He downed his glass in a single gulp, then looked over at Fitna and said, "We once had joint projects in mind!"

She nodded in agreement, and he continued, "So what's to prevent us from carrying them out?"

"That's for you to say," she replied evenly.

Pointing to her husband, she said, "He was also part of the projects." Then she added confidently, "He'll have a respectable role, and I'd like first to study his role in the script."

"Great. However, I'd advise you to exercise flexibility and good judgment. Producing a film in these dismal circumstances is an adventure, and those who undertake it deserve full appreciation. At any moment, as the result of an attack or raid, work on a film, and possibly even the entire film industry, could grind to a halt. It's the prudent producer who understands this."

With calm determination she said, "I've said what I think, Mr. Ridwan."

"Remember that our personal concerns are nothing by comparison with the woes being suffered by the country!"

Laughing in spite of herself, she said, "I don't remember you being concerned about such woes in the past!"

"Is this the way someone talks to a man whose brother is working on the front?" he protested.

Thereupon he rose, bowed again in farewell, and departed.

33

Aliyat had met Hamid in Mona Zahran's house in Zamalek, where she'd been invited for dinner at Mona's along with Saniya and Aliyat. Hamid was the brother of Salim, Mona's husband. From the very beginning Hamid had been impressed with Aliyat. So, as he was giving her and Saniya a ride to the bus station, he announced his desire to see Aliyat again and get to know her better. Saniya encouraged the idea, so it was agreed upon. The two of them met in the late afternoon in Talaat Harb Square, and he asked her where she'd like them to sit. She suggested that they go to Dar al-Shay al-Hindi, perhaps because she remembered how it had brought Mona and Salim together. He already had quite a bit of information about her, such as her academic degree, her job at the Ministry of Social Affairs, and other facts which she assumed that Mona had passed on to him. However, she was amazed to hear him tell her about his humble position as a clerical worker, which was inconsistent with his intelligent, sophisticated manner of speaking.

"What did you major in?" she asked him.

Somewhat uncomfortably he replied, "All I have is a high school diploma!"

A bit flustered, she said, "But you're very cultured!"

"That's another matter," he said.

In her eyes he could see questions that she was concealing with her good manners, so he said, "As soon as I finished high school, I was arrested."

"Why?" she asked, her tone registering concern.

"I'd been accused of being a communist!" he laughed.

She looked at him with a combination of sympathy and curiosity, and he continued, "Actually, I wasn't a communist when I was arrested for being one."

"That's as unfortunate as it is strange."

"It's as strange as you are beautiful," he replied with a smile.

She thought to herself: How many times have I heard those words? And how many times have they been uttered about the beauty of my face alone?

"Don't exaggerate," she said.

"From the first time I saw you, I had a feeling there would be something between us."

"Thank you," she said simply.

Resuming her questioning, she asked, "But how did you come to be accused of being a communist?"

"I don't know."

"I never imagined that mistakes could be made so easily."

"Anything's possible," he said derisively.

A look of scorn and bitterness appeared in her honey-colored eyes.

"I was eight years old when the revolution began, so I inherited its after-effects."

They exchanged a long look, after which he said, "My brother's wife Mona admires you. She's also told me about your brother, the hero."

"He's making his way in the darkness with a strong will."

"She's also inspired my admiration for his wife."

"Sometimes love elevates us to new spiritual heights."

"I think that's always the case."

"No, not always."

"There's no need for pessimism, which I hate."

"All right."

They sipped tea and between the two of them ate four pieces of cake, all the while exchanging suggestive glances.

Then she asked him, "Have you been drafted?"

"No," he replied tersely. Then he added, "I can hardly see out of my left eye."

"Is it on account of an illness?" she asked sympathetically.

"I nearly lost it while I was in prison."

A look of terror etched itself on her face, and he said with a smile, "I could admire you with just one eye. How much more so, then, with one and a quarter!"

"Yet in spite of it all, you're innocent of the charge of communism!"

"When they released me, I'd become a communist in their eyes," he replied lightheartedly.

She laughed, and so did he. Things seemed enormously comical to both of them.

Then he asked her, "What would you prefer? Dancing, or a movie?"

"Not tonight, please," she said sweetly.

34

After greeting the visitor with a look of surprise, Husni Higgawi opened his arms and the two of them embraced warmly. Then she loosed himself from his embrace and went before him to the sitting room as he said to her, "My dear Samra Wagdi, what a pleasure . . . ."

She switched off the radio, and as she did so she asked him, "Were you listening to the latest news on the raids? I'm dying for one of your cocktails."

"This is the first time you've come by yourself!" he said as he made his way to the bar.

As she took her glass, she replied smoothly, "This time I'm coming for my own sake, not for yours."

Of medium stature, lithe as a circus performer, and graced with a fair but rosy complexion, she exhibited an elegant, regal beauty from the front and from the left. As for the right side of her face, it was taut, shrunken, and tanned a blackish red. It was marred further by unsightly spots and tumorous-looking bumps. She sat down and crossed her legs, all the while looking at him with an air of inscrutability and expectancy that piqued his curiosity to the limit.

Standing before her, he said, "I'm delighted to see you, Samra!"

"Don't lie," she replied. "What makes you happy are the little birds I bring you."

"But you know how much I love and respect you."

"I don't care about respect!" she said acerbically.

"Nothing refines a human being like tragedy."

"Don't remind me of things I've forgotten."

With an air of truthfulness he replied, "We live in a depraved age in which people worship wealth. You could be making thousands in profits, but instead you give lavishly for the sake of amusement and love, not money. You're from another planet."

She laughed with pleasure and said, "I'm a store proprietor, and rich."

"Don't be so modest. If you wanted to, you could become far richer than you are."

She rose and went to the bar uninvited to refill her glass, then returned to her seat, saying, "Listen, my dear dirty old man, I've come to see you about a personal concern."

"I'm at your service. Perhaps you'd like to see my latest flicks?"

With a look that penetrated to his depths, she said coolly, "I want Aliyat."

He appeared at first to be trying to recall who she was referring to.

"The girl you called on me to perform an abortion for," she said sharply.

"Ah," he said, "but I hardly know anything about her, and I wouldn't be able to find out more unless she came to me on her own. Might I presume to ask why you want her?"

"I seem to be in love with her," she said plainly.

"And would she welcome that?" he asked with a chuckle.

"I'm hopeful that she would."

"Don't you have enough girls to . . . ?"

"What is this nonsense?" she broke in impetuously. "I wouldn't expect to hear such a thing from a tried-and-true libertine like yourself!"

"My apologies. But she was with you, wasn't she?"

"She dropped by the shop once to thank me, then she disappeared."

"Maybe she disappeared on purpose."

"How can I contact her?"

"I promise to let her know of your wishes if she comes to see me."

"You're no help!" she retorted. "You're just selfish. You want to take, but you don't want to give, and you forget all I've done for you!"

"I once tried to hook you up with a wonderful man."

"You know very well that I don't like men, so don't go fishing for gratitude from me!"

He reflected a bit, then said, "I know, for example, that she's an employee at the Ministry of Social Affairs, but I don't know which branch she works in. I don't know her address, either. Sometimes news about her reaches me through her father, who works as a waiter at the Inshirah coffeeshop on Sheikh Qamar Street."

"I'll be waiting for a call from you."

They exchanged a long look, then he said with a smile, "Drink up, my dear!"

35

Dark clouds of anxiety and unspoken fears hung over life. This, at least, is what Marzouq Anwar felt, and Fitna shared his sentiments, though she pretended otherwise. The fact that they enjoyed the outward trappings of an extravagant life studded with resounding laughter and the clinking of glasses in toasts to one another's health didn't change a thing. And the more polite, genteel words were spoken, the greater the wariness and apprehension became, sullying life's joy from their unseen haunts.

One day Marzouq said to her, "Contract season is over now, and we didn't land a single one!"

Making light of the matter, she said, "Let it be a year's vacation, then."

Reading her unspoken thoughts and aware of what was being said by those around them, he said, "Things can't go on this way."

"Let them go on however they like," she said obdurately.

That's the tenacity of the warrior, not love, he thought to himself. And how am I to know whether love even exists as anything but the armor around the warrior's hard heart? After all, the person she fell in love with doesn't exist anymore.

"It won't do for us to wait till we've gone bankrupt together."

"You worry too much. The world is a much nicer place than you imagine it to be."

"I hope you won't reject any more work on my account in the future."

"Even if it's with Ahmad Ridwan?"

"Even if it's with Ahmad Ridwan."

"But I'm determined!"

"I refuse!" he cried in desperation.

"Would you accept some secondary role?"

"It wouldn't be any better than an ordinary job."

Troubled, she said, "Tell me what you really feel."

"You could work in your field and let me go back to my original line of work."

Wrapping her arms around his neck and kissing him on the cheek, she said, "You're the victim of my love!"

Concealing his indignation, he said, "There's no place for sympathy here."

"But I love you first and last!" she said reproachfully.

He kissed her on her cheek, then said, "Listen to me. I've lost my taste for acting."

Deeply affected, she looked away from him.

"That doesn't matter at all to me anymore," she insisted.

She fell silent for a while, then said, "What really matters is our love."

"It's madness for us to crawl if we could fly!"

"What do you mean?"

He made no reply. He clenched his jaw, thereby bringing out the false severity in his features.

"You're so paranoid!"

"Beware of pity," he said with a smile.

"Stop saying that word!" she cried irritably.

"Your wish is my command."

"Situations that have no solution are so miserable," she said with a sigh.

"Every situation, no matter how complex it is, has a solution."

"Yes, but it may be at the expense of one's dignity, happiness, or both."

"It's still better than inaction that paralyzes the will."

"I disagree."

Exasperated, he said, "We've got to recognize that we haven't found the happiness we'd dreamed of."

"You're insulting me!" she shouted, her tone heralding a flow of tears.

"There's nothing insulting about what I said."

"That's what *you* think!"

"We had wanted to mount wings on our shared body, but they've turned into crutches!"

"All I wanted was to marry the man I loved," she said defiantly.

"Please accept my apologies," he said, and gave her a perfunctory kiss.

Then he got up, saying, "I'm going out for a walk."

105

"At this hour of the night?"

"At this hour, walking is good medicine," he replied as he strode out the door.

36

They were smoking in the stillness of the night, enveloped in a comfortable silence. Husni Higgawi was engaged in a private conversation with the tobacco smoke he was puffing out in a leisurely rhythm. Abduh Badran was smoking a cigarette, and so was Ashmawi, who was crouching near the warmth of the stove. Outside one could hear the voices of Sufi adepts commemorating the birthdate of Sidi al-Bayyumi.

A taamiya vendor came up carrying a stuffed round of pita bread with some sprigs of parsley dangling from its edges and handed it to Ashmawi. He stood there waiting for the money while Ashmawi with his hazy vision fumbled for some coins in a tin can.

The taamiya vendor said to him, "Our men infiltrated enemy lines yesterday and destroyed them."

Ashmawi nodded exultantly and the man went on, "And after that the army will advance!"

As he gave him the coins, Ashmawi said, "And don't forget our air attacks. It's our turn now."

The man went away satisfied, and Ashmawi proceeded to eat his food, smacking his lips audibly to the accompaniment of the gurgling of the shisha.

Ashmawi turned to Husni Higgawi and said, "They've brought him a three-wheeled cart that he can sit in and propel with his hands. But he doesn't go out very far by himself."

At first Husni Higgawi didn't know who he was talking about.

Then he remembered the story of Ashmawi's neighbor whose legs had been amputated.

"Marvelous, marvelous," he replied.

"Will he be able to get married, Ashmawi?" asked Abduh Badran.

"Yes. I found that out from his grandmother!"

"A wife like that will earn a reward," added Husni Higgawi. "A person can get used to anything but loneliness."

"Ibrahim is facing life with determination and success," said Amm Abduh.

"You're educated, and that's a big advantage," Ashmawi commented.

With his usual crude candor, he went on to compare blindness with losing one's legs. Then he sighed, saying, "When I was a young man, if I walked down a street, the Jews would go running for cover."

Unable to contain himself, Husni Higgawi laughed until he started to cough. Then they fell silent, and once again they could hear the singers' voices wafting in their direction.

"I used to be one of al-Bayyumi's disciples."

"You've been a crook all your life. What have you got to do with spiritual paths!" retorted Amm Abduh.

The old man guffawed and made no comment. Then Amm Abduh sidled up to Husni Higgawi like someone who's got a secret to tell. An expert at reading his moods, Husni asked him what he had on his mind.

"Aliyat's been proposed to by a good man," he said.

"Really?" the man murmured in a tone of satisfaction.

"He's a young man who works for the government, and his brother's a senior judge."

"God bless them."

Amm Abduh kept quiet for a while, pensive and hesitant. Then he said, "I've been told he was in prison!"

"So, do they hire ex-cons these days?" Ashmawi broke in.

" . . . for political reasons," continued Amm Abduh.

Husni said, "There's nothing dishonorable about it, Ashmawi."

"And Ibrahim approves of him," added Amm Abduh. "If there were something dishonorable about it, he would never have agreed."

"I was a political prisoner once," said Ashmawi.

"Once!" retorted Abduh, "And then dozens of times after that for reasons that had nothing to do with politics!"

"If you want to know the truth, there's nothing dishonorable about drugs, either!"

"Then what about beatings and assaults?"

"They're what it takes to be a good racketeer!" he replied smugly.

"Damn you!" Abduh exclaimed with a laugh.

Clapping his hands, Ashmawi said, "What's the world coming to?! Naked women in the streets, ex-cons getting jobs, and Jews invading our country!"

Then they fell silent again and went on listening to the singers.

37

Aliyat was on duty at the ministry one day when she was visited, unannounced, by a woman who worked in Samra Wagdi's shop. The woman began by telling her what a terrible time she'd had locating her, after which she invited her to meet Samra in her shop on Sherif Street. Aliyat tensed up inside. She hadn't forgotten the favor Samra had done her, and she had paid her a visit in the shop once to thank her. However, she'd noticed at the time that Samra seemed unusually anxious to cement their relationship, and in a way that aroused her suspicion.

Consequently, she'd never thought of visiting her again, and she cringed inside at the latest invitation.

Samra was a bundle of contradictions. On one hand, she had a stately appearance and wasn't the least bit greedy or materialistic. On the other hand, she'd lived a dissolute life and was on intimate terms with that doctor whose clinic bore an uncanny resemblance to an autopsy room. One evening she went to see Husni Higgawi, told him the story of the invitation, and talked to him about her assorted qualms and forebodings.

The man was flustered at first. Then, with that straightforwardness of his that could sometimes be frightening, he said, "Samra is in love with you!"

There was only one way she could take his words despite the fact that they might have borne more than one interpretation, and she was genuinely alarmed.

However, she decided to play dumb.

"What do you mean?" she asked.

"You know exactly what I mean."

She furrowed her brow and pursed her lips.

"Don't you have any experience in such things?" he asked gently.

"No," she replied in disgust.

"So, then, there will be problems!"

"Problems?" she murmured fearfully.

He gave her a quick rundown on Samra Wagdi, past and present. Then he said, "She's a world of misery, adventure, and fun all wrapped into one."

"I'm not going," she said, her voice sounding fretful.

Then she added imploringly, "You can protect me from anything!"

"I'll try," he assured her, "but I'm not sure what will come of my efforts."

True to his sense of responsibility, he invited Samra to come see him. Upon her arrival, he served her a drink mixed with his engaging humor. As for her, she eyed him the entire time with a penetrating gaze from beneath her long lashes.

"Get to the point!" she said shrewdly.

Laughing out loud, he said, "Your friend isn't that type!"

"She didn't respond to my invitation."

"She came to me instead."

"Did you lay it on the line with her?"

"She isn't that type," he repeated with affable discretion. "She's also about to get married. So put your sights elsewhere."

In an outburst of rage, she cried, "The disgusting little ingrate!"

"Samra!"

"If I get angry . . . ."

"But there's no reason to be angry."

"That's for me to decide."

Caressing her chin with his fingers, he asked, "Do you think you can force someone to do what she doesn't want to?"

"The filthy little beast. Has she forgotten?"

"Samra, Aliyat went through a bitter experience just the way you did once. And now she's about to get married."

"She'll never get married."

Appalled by her decree, he said, "But you're not cruel or evil."

"You don't know me yet, then."

"So what do you intend to do, my dear?"

"I'm going to tell her fiancé all about her."

"No!" he cried.

"Yes."

"I don't believe it."

"You'll see."

Defeated, he fell silent for some time.

Then he said, "You let your first tormenter off scot-free!"

"I was green."

Turning away from her hopelessly, Husni headed for the bar.

38

Marzouq Anwar had disappeared and no one had found a trace of him. He'd done his deed and vanished. Once gone, he had sentenced himself to near-total solitary confinement in a boarding house in Helwan. From his place of confinement he followed the news about himself in arts magazines, and the news was curious indeed: "Marzouq flees from conjugal nest, then sends Fitna Nadir a writ of divorce and a heart-rending letter." "Fitna suffers a nervous breakdown and is treated by physicians." "Fitna searches high and low for her divorced husband, but finds no trace of him."

After some time the furor died down and news about the incident was drowned in a sea of other events. Still more time passed, and there were reports that Fitna had agreed to work on a new film being directed by Ahmad Ridwan. Marzouq thought to himself: I'm as good as dead. However, I've gotten to do what no dead man before me has ever had a chance to, namely, witness what he's left behind by way of existence and nonexistence. And now I've got two options before me: either the life of a loyal dog, or that of a pimp.

When the dust had settled, he went back to his family and decided to get a job.

Then one day when Aliyat was in her office at the ministry, who should visit her unannounced but Marzouq himself. She looked intently into his face for an entire half-minute as though she were in doubt as to his identity, which pained him no end.

He said to her, "I had no choice but to come."

She didn't understand what he meant, and it was clear to him that she was uncomfortable with his visit. But he said, "I'd like to apologize so that I can go on with my life."

Keeping her emotions in check, she said, "It doesn't matter."

Rather than leaving, he sat down and said, "Let's have lunch together. There are some things I'd like to say."

"There's no point in it," she said coolly.

"I insist."

Seeing that he was in a fragile condition that called for a compassionate response, she relented. They went to the older branch of al-Kursal and had lunch, though neither had an appetite. Then he ordered coffee.

Pointing to his face, he said, "This is what I've come to."

Keeping her face expressionless by an act of the will, she said softly, "It was a stroke of really bad luck. But it can be overcome."

"Thanks."

"There's no need to lose hope. Think of the example of my brother Ibrahim."

He thanked her again. He sensed that there was a kind of inaccessibility about her that enclosed her spirit like a fortress, and after some thought, he said, "You must be angry with me."

With an uncompromising directness she said, "That's over and done with."

Smiling unthinkingly, he said to her, "That makes it even worse."

She made no reply.

He said, "Sometimes we commit crimes under the sway of a madness that has no meaning."

"But it does have a meaning," she objected.

In a tone he'd learned from his time as an actor—though he spoke truthfully—he said, "I'd been thinking that the punishment that's been meted out to me might help me find forgiveness."

"I don't know what you're talking about."

After a long hesitation, he said, "Can I hope for your forgiveness?"

"I don't know what you're asking for."

"But it's obvious."

"It doesn't matter anymore."

"But to me, it's everything."

"I repeat: It doesn't matter anymore."

With a hopeful glimmer in his eyes, he said, "It might open a new page for us."

"What new page?" she asked resolutely.

"You know exactly what I mean!"

"Don't waste your time," she replied in a definitive tone.

"Listen to me . . . ."

"I refuse even to think about it."

"Let's wait until your anger subsides."

"I'm not angry. Believe me. But I'm getting ready to open another new page."

Then she showed him her engagement ring.

"Really?" he murmured.

"I'll be getting married soon."

Silence reigned until at last he asked, "Is your decision final?"

"Of course."

Then she got up, saying, "It's time for me to be going."

She left alone, and as she walked away, she experienced an overwhelming relief. She felt liberated and victorious. As evidence of her triumph, she harbored no bitterness or ill will toward him, and she felt no malicious glee over his misfortune. She thought to herself: It's completely dead. How amazing.

39

Aliyat was sitting with Hamid in Dar al-Shay al-Hindi one day when who should appear all of a sudden but Samra Wagdi, standing at the edge of their table. Aliyat went pale as the blood drained out of her face. Taken aback, Hamid looked back and forth in bewilderment between the two women. He started to say something, but Samra beat him to the punch.

With the stench of alcohol on her breath, she said to Aliyat, "I'm stubborn, as you can see."

"What's going on?" asked Hamid.

"First invite me to sit down as decency requires," she said to him.

In the woman's attitude he perceived a subtle danger that threatened their well-being.

"But I haven't had the pleasure of meeting you."

Taking a seat, she said insolently, "So, I'll sit down without an invitation, then."

Then she let loose a laugh which, against the staid tranquility of the place, was sure to sound obnoxious.

Hamid said to her, "Your behavior is inappropriate, Madam."

"But your fiancée knows me," she replied acerbically, "and I've come to complain to you about her."

Moved by Aliyat's vulnerable state, he said, "I still consider your behavior inappropriate."

Ignoring his objection, she replied, "What I've come to complain about is that I once performed an invaluable service for your girl, and all I got in return was ingratitude."

At this point Aliyat nearly slapped her. However, for fear of unforeseen complications, she let cowardice get the better of her, and found herself unable even to speak.

"What do you want?" Hamid demanded furiously.

"First we'll talk about the service, and I'll leave it to you to calculate the price," she rejoined with vulgar insolence.

"Criminal," muttered Aliyat. "You're a criminal."

"Shame on you!" said Samra with a cruel laugh.

Enraged, Hamid said, "If you please. I don't allow . . . ."

Samra interrupted him with a cough.

114

"Imagine a girl from a working-class family who accidentally finds herself with child, and who . . . ."

"Leave, please," he said heatedly.

However, she went right on talking.

"How could you imagine the depths of her misery? And how could you possibly put a price on the service provided by someone who sets her free from the unborn child and restores her honor?"

Speechless with rage, Hamid began pointing his finger at her menacingly.

"It would be better for you to go," he said.

"Are you threatening me?"

"Yes, I am."

"What do you think, Aliyat?" she queried mockingly.

Aliyat didn't utter a word. As for Hamid, he just sat there glowering, speechless with rage and indignation.

It was clear that he was in the grip of a violent rage. Convinced that she had hit the mark and accomplished her mission to a tee, Samra began to get up under the influence of a sudden fearfulness. By this time, however, Hamid had gotten hold of his emotions, passing beyond his crisis, and had come out impassive, unyielding, and determined.

He asked the woman, "Are you the person who performed this service?"

She nodded her head in the affirmative.

Then he asked her daringly, "For Aliyat?"

Again she nodded.

Fully in command of his nerves, he said, "I owe you a word of thanks. What price are you asking?"

She scrutinized him attentively to see how serious or angry he really was.

Again he asked her evenly, "What price are you asking?"

Suddenly she felt distraught and befuddled.

"It seems you don't want anything," he concluded. "That being the case, I ask you please to vacate the premises so that we can go on with our conversation!"

She rose to her feet unsteadily, then departed in a huff.

On the verge of total collapse, Aliyat rested her head on her hand and closed her eyes in exhaustion.

He looked at her sorrowfully without saying a word. He could feel the storm raging in her heart, and, leaning toward her sympathetically, said, "What do you say we take a walk in the fresh air?"

Raising her head, she said in hopeless resignation, "Hamid . . . ."

"There's no need to say anything," he interrupted her gently. "We need some fresh air."

40

Contrary to his usual relaxed state, Husni Higgawi had a knot in his stomach during the peaceful nighttime session at the Inshirah coffeeshop. Releasing his pent-up anxiety into the shisha, he took one puff after another in rapid succession until the coals blazed red-hot while the tobacco burned and began giving off an unpleasant odor. He kept expecting Amm Abduh Badran to come out with the sad story that Aliyat's engagement had been called off. Instead, though, he just stood there smoking a cigarette as he leaned against the wall's wooden paneling. His eyes were fixed in a heavy, opaque look, as though he was getting drowsy. Perhaps he was just waiting for an opportunity to confide his woes. And when he did, Husni Higgawi would find himself in the heart of a tragedy for the first time in his life. Consequently, he avoided looking in Amm Abduh's direction.

Ashmawi, who was squatting near the stove, had come down with a cold and wasn't chattering away in his accustomed fashion. He had the look of an old man about to breathe his last.

Detecting the smell of the burning tobacco, Amm Abduh came up and said, "Shall I wet the tobacco for you?"

"Change it," replied Husni, suddenly aware of the bad-tempered treatment to which he'd been subjecting the shisha.

The man took the shisha away and replaced the tobacco, then brought it back filled with new tobacco that looked bright as a handful of gold nuggets.

"Marzouq Anwar paid us a visit with Saniya and Ibrahim!" he said.

Sensing that things might be all right after all, Husni replied with sudden enthusiasm, "That was audacious of him!"

"He apologized, and he congratulated me on Aliyat's new engagement."

"It's a noble thing to forgive."

"He's found a job in the Transport Company, and he's going to study for a graduate degree."

Awash in relief, Husni said, "It's a lovely thing for a person to start all over again."

"His first and last hope now is to be able to emigrate."

"Emigrating is all the rage these days. We're living in strange times."

He thought to himself: Aliyat must be fine. Samra's arrow must have missed its mark. And he felt grateful to those with mentalities that change with the times.

Encouraged, he asked him, "So, how's our bride doing?"

"Her fiancé wants them to get married as soon as possible," said Amm Abduh.

"With God's blessing!"

"But I can't offer her anything worth mentioning," the man said forlornly.

"That's all right."

Just then he heard something stirring at the door. He turned his head, and who should he see but Samra Wagdi, standing there still as a statue. Amm Abduh looked at her in astonishment. Ashmawi looked up, squinting, then his jaw dropped. Husni's heart skipped a beat, and his hair stood on end.

"Incredible," he muttered absently.

She shot him a cold, menacing glance, then shifted her gaze defiantly away from him.

Looking at Amm Abduh, she said, "Amm Abduh Badran?"

Dazzled by her sumptuous, elegant appearance, the man came up to her politely in response to her query.

"Yes, Madam?" he said.

With all eyes upon her, she proceeded toward the far corner of the coffeeshop, and he followed her without hesitation. To his horror, Husni Higgawi had deduced what was behind her visit, and, feeling that he was about to suffocate, he remembered that it was through directions he had given her unintentionally that she had found her way to the place. He, himself, then, was the axis of the mill that was crushing a group of people for whom he had never felt anything but affection and good will. Some evil was about to descend upon all, but by what wisdom could it be averted? If he intervened, it would mean exposing himself, which would lead ultimately to the exposure of his magic abode. On the other hand, would the danger be averted if he remained a mere onlooker? Thereupon he loosed himself from his paralysis—or so it seemed to him—and opened his mouth to speak.

"The woman's drunk and out of her mind!" he warned.

But no one heard him. Not a sound came out from his mouth. His strength gave out on him and he just sat there, impotent. At the same time, he didn't take his eyes off the couple in the corner. He listened closely, but he couldn't hear a word of what was being said. The woman was whispering while the man listened with rapt attention. Ashmawi was looking and listening, too, but to no avail. Husni Higgawi could feel the place where they were sitting begin to rock and sway, then sink into the ground while his magic nest went flying through the air on the wings of the angels of death.

He focused his gaze on Amm Abduh Badran's face. He was listening, and from time to time his lips would move. The heavy look in his eyes became gloomier, he furrowed his brow, and his face clouded over. Then suddenly his head reeled backward as though he had received a heavy blow to the face. The cigarette fell out of his hand, his eyes flashed, and out of his mouth there came the guttural moan of an animal being put to the slaughter. He staggered like a drunk man. Then suddenly he lunged at the woman, took hold of her neck with both hands, and squeezed with all his might.

"No!" Husni shouted in alarm.

As he jumped frantically to his feet, his knee bumped up against the shisha, sending it tumbling to the floor.

Ashmawi got up, too, crying, "What happened?"

The two men went rushing over to Amm Abduh.

"Get hold of yourself, Amm Abduh!" Husni pleaded.

However, by the time the man released his iron grip, the woman was a lifeless corpse.

41

"Did you strangle this woman?"

"Yes."

"Why did you strangle her?"

" . . . "

"Why did you strangle her?"

". . ."

"What was your relationship to her?"

"I didn't know her."

"Are you saying you didn't know her?"

"I'd never seen her before that terrible day."

"So why did you strangle her?"

". . ."

"Did you strangle her for no reason?"

". . ."

"What did she say to you?"

"Your silence means that you're delivering yourself to the gallows."

". . ."

Amm Abduh Badran insisted on remaining silent.

Meanwhile, through Ashmawi's testimony there emerged a picture of Samra Wagdi's sudden appearance; her looking at Amm Abduh Badran and saying, "Amm Abduh Badran?"; Husni Higgawi's saying, "Incredible"; the woman's repairing to the far corner of the coffeeshop with Amm Abduh; the conversation of which he hadn't heard a word; and the crime which no one had been able to prevent.

"Did she call out to Amm Abduh, or was she asking about him?"

"She looked at him and asked, 'Amm Abduh Badran?'"

"So, then, she didn't know him."

"That's the way it seems, and that's all I can say."

"Do you have any idea how she happened to come to him?"

"No."

"Or what they talked about?"

"I didn't hear a word."

"How much do you know about your friend's relationships with women?"

"For shame! He's a good-hearted, unlucky man who's always lived a pure life."

"How do you explain his having committed this crime?"

"I don't know. He'd never hurt a flea before this. Only God knows why he did it!"

"Why did Husni Higgawi say, 'Incredible'?"

"I don't know. But for a beautiful woman to show up at the Inshirah coffeeshop after midnight *is* incredible."

"Do you think he knew her?"

"They didn't say anything to each other, and that's all I know."

Husni Higgawi's testimony shed no new light on events. The investigator asked him, "Why did you say, 'Incredible'?"

"It was incredible that she would come to the Inshirah at that hour."

"Had you ever seen her before?"

"Yes. I know her superficially, since she owns a shop on the street where I live."

"Could you specify what kind of knowledge you have of her?"

"I only know her in passing."

"But the two of you didn't even exchange a cursory greeting."

"I expected that we would, but she completely ignored me."

"How do you explain that?"

"Maybe she was preoccupied with the concern that had brought her to the coffeeshop."

"What was there between her and Amm Abduh in your opinion?"

"Nothing at all."

"What did they talk about?"

"I didn't hear a word."

"What's your explanation of the crime?"

"It's beyond belief, and I have no explanation for it."

"What do you know about the deceased?"

"I know nothing about her private affairs."

"How do you explain the silence of the accused?"

"It's a mystery. I don't know what to make of it."

42

Policemen are demons. They know how to make life hell on earth and they breathe fire into pallid faces. They knock politely on people's doors as though they were coming as friends, then storm their houses like a hurricane. A middle-aged man stands before them stripped of his dignity, his heart so gripped with fear that he concludes that life is nothing but illusion and loss. They ransack walls, mattresses, pockets, and closets until joys and dreams vanish into thin air. When that happens, he walks among them without legs, without eyes, without a tomorrow, and with an infernal murmur ringing in his ears. And if he has any life left in him, he cries with a rattle in his throat, "I'm a goner!"

"Your name?"

"Husni Higgawi."

"Your age?"

"Fifty."

"Your profession?"

"Cinematographer."

"Do you admit to being the owner of these films?"

"Yes, I do."

"And that you've showed them to scores of underage girls?"

"Yes."

"And that you've had sex with them?"

"Yes."

"Do you still stand by what you said about the passing nature of your relationship with Samra Wagdi?"

"No. She was actually an old friend."

"Did she used to bring girls to you to watch your pornographic films?"

"Yes, she did."

"What is your relationship to Aliyat, the daughter of the accused, Abduh Badran?"

"She used to be a friend."

"Wasn't she a lover of yours as well at one time?"

"Yes, she was."

"Do you admit that you facilitated an abortion for her?"

"Yes."

"How?"

"I went to Samra Wagdi for help."

"Did Samra admit to you that she was in love with Aliyat?"

"Yes."

"Did she seek out your help in satisfying her wicked craving?"

"Yes, but I tried to keep her away from her."

"Did you give her a lead as to Abduh Badran's whereabouts?"

"She asked me where Aliyat worked, and I told her that I didn't know exactly where she worked, though I knew she was an employee at the Ministry of Social Affairs. I told her that I hardly had any dealings with her anymore and that I would only learn of her news by chance at the Inshirah coffeeshop, where her father works as a waiter. I never imagined that she would pay him the bizarre visit that led to her death."

"And why did she pay him that bizarre visit?"

"She was determined to get back at Aliyat for not responding to her shameless overtures. As a consequence, she barged in on her one day while she was sitting with her fiancé and, in Aliyat's hearing, told him about the abortion. Then, when she saw that she'd failed to accomplish what she'd hoped to in this way, she made another attempt with the girl's father, and he killed her."

"Do you think this was the real motive behind Amm Abduh's crime?"

"There's no other possible motive in my opinion."

"Do you have anything else to say?"

"No."

Husni Higgawi was out driving at dawn along the outskirts of the city. His nerves were so on edge, slumber was a distant hope, and he was haunted constantly by the specters of his imagination. Inquiries would be made about Samra Wagdi, and they were bound eventually to reveal a world replete with madness and curiosities. He was well-versed in such matters. Before long everything would be out in the open, and the investigation would sweep scores of young women into its net. Soon the raging storm would sweep over his happy, enchanted nest, and he would be led away in handcuffs. He wondered what sorts of pictures, telephone numbers, and names would be found in Samra Wagdi's house. Had she recorded her adventures in a journal? Would he be summoned for questioning? Would he be thrown in prison? Would he commit suicide? Was there any way out?

43

Aliyat and Hamid met at Dar al-Shay al-Hindi. Her nerves were spent, and her eyes red. He was marshaling his inmost resources to face the situation, but his heart was filled with unnamed fears.

"My father . . . my father," she repeated. "We've got to save him!"

"That's surely what we hope to do, but how?"

"At any price," she said, her voice filled with steely resolve.

"We'll do all we can and more."

"We know everything."

"That's right. And he insists on remaining silent in order to protect your reputation."

"I'll never desert him," she said, muffling a sob.

"We won't abandon him to a terrible punishment he doesn't deserve."

Casting him a tearful glance, she said, "That means we have to testify to what we know."

"There's no other way."

"But will they believe us?"

"In my opinion, we should bring the case to Hasan Hammouda and consult him about the matter before we make our testimony."

"All right."

"So, the way is clear."

Biting her lip, she murmured, "The secret will be out now."

"Yes."

"And that will mean problems."

"Perhaps," he said apprehensively.

"I'm making a sacrifice to save my father, but I'll be dragging you along with me."

"I don't agree with your way of thinking," he objected.

"I don't want to burden you with more than you can bear."

His heart quailed at the anticipated consequences. But he said, "That's my business."

Then, lowering her head, she said, "You have no obligations . . . "

"Aliyat!" he interrupted her forcefully. "What's this nonsense?!"

As he mustered his will to crush his hesitation, his heart sank. However, he mocked and despised his fears.

Then, casting himself upon the unknown with a granite-like resolve, he said, "I'll never leave you."

44

For the first time ever the room was immersed in an all-embracing gloom. Husni Higgawi and Aliyat sat facing each other, separated by a short distance. They exchanged dull, cold glances as though they were statues of gods, or stuffed animals on a shelf. Abandoned for the first time by his jocular, expansive spirit, the man found himself crushed by name-less entities that were closing in on the room from an unknown world.

He said to her, "I asked about you everywhere."

"I was coming on my own anyway," she replied flatly.

Her response penetrated to the depths of his spirit, and he said uneasily, "I'm always at your service."

"I've been advised to hire the services of Hasan Hammouda."

Pressing his nostrils in with his fingers as he brooded, Husni said, "He's a top notch criminal lawyer."

Her voice slightly lower, she said, "I've heard his fees are exorbitant."

"You'll find everything you need at your disposal," he replied with a sigh of relief.

"I don't know how to thank you."

Taking her hand in his, he said, "Aliyat, haven't I always been the best of friends?"

She nodded her head in affirmation as a tear trickled down her cheek and landed on her knee.

"I have a request to make of you," he said.
"What's that?"
He remained silent for an entire minute. Then he said,

"That you not mention my name either to the lawyer or during the investigation."

"There would no point in it as far as I can tell," she replied, drying her eyes.

"Precisely," he said, a joyous sense of hope welling up in his soul. "After all, it wouldn't do any good, and as you know, it could hurt me."

"I wouldn't do anything to hurt you."

"Thank you. You might say that you met Samra in her shop and that she tried to draw you into a lesbian relationship but you refused, and that after that she wanted to get back at you, etc., etc."

"That's the truth in a nutshell."

He kissed her hand and said, "Do what you need to do, then, and don't worry about the money."

For a few minutes after she'd left, he felt he'd been relieved of his burden and that life's current had begun surging anew through his heart, unhindered and carefree. Am I really off the hook? he wondered. If I am, then nothing can hurt me for as long as I live. However, his euphoria was short-lived. It was buried alive without warning as his logical mind went back to work exuding its deadly toxins. What difference would Aliyat's promise make? He wondered. What could she do to escape the siege of interrogations? And would her testimony be of any use without support from an eyewitness, like him, who had been at the center of events and their prime mover? And then there were the inquiries that were stirring to life everywhere now like ravenous wolves. No. No. There was no safety for him. He would have to flee, and at the earliest opportunity. He had promised to shoot a film in Lebanon, so he would apply to travel right away before his name came up in the investigation. Then he would settle in Lebanon forever. There was no life for him in this country.

Farewell, Egypt!

45

What a bombshell! Do things like this really happen in life? Imagine him, of all people, being invited to defend the person who had killed Samra Wagdi! He cast his gaze back and forth between Aliyat and Hamid, concealing his agitation behind a cool façade of detachment.

He said, "I've read what's been published about the crime in the newspapers, and I've given a lot of thought to how to explain the secret behind the accused man's silence."

"We know all the secrets," said Hamid.

"Pardon me," he replied hurriedly, "but you should keep them to yourself. I haven't accepted the case yet."

"But you *will* accept it, won't you?" interjected Aliyat.

Ah, Samra Wagdi! thought Hasan Hammouda. Why do you suppose the man murdered her? On account of some scandal, no doubt.

Defending him would require that the lawyer concerned dig into the woman's past, unearth her scandals, and spread them abroad. So should he be the one to do it? And if he did, could he rule out the possibility that some unnamed individual might set out to reveal his own deep, dark secret, thereby exposing the scandalous part he once played in this woman's life?

Without hesitation he replied, "I'm sorry, but I have no time."

"But surely you're not going to leave us in the lurch!" cried Aliyat.

"Professional considerations require me to refuse the case. However, I'll pass it on to a well-known colleague of mine whose reputation is beyond dispute."

"But you're the one we've come to!"

In a polite but definitive tone he said, "Professional and moral considerations alone prevent me from taking it."

Aliyat was about to speak again when Hamid leaned toward her, saying, "We have to believe him and thank him. These are obstacles to be overcome, but the way has been prepared now for what we hope to do."

When Hasan Hammouda was alone again, the mask of cool composure he had been hiding behind fell to pieces. He sank into his chair and began staring at the white ceiling in a daze. Strange fears emerged before him like dancing ghosts, and he was gripped by a feeling that he was being pursued. Jumping out of his chair as if it were responsible for his weakness, he began pacing around the room and saying in a loud voice as if to drive the ghosts away, "They're nothing but illusions! It's just a dead past, and the dead don't come back to life!"

Hating to be alone at that moment, he left the office. He got in his car and went driving about aimlessly for an hour. Then he felt an urge to see Safwat Morgan, so he pointed his car in the direction of Ahmad Shawqi Street for an unannounced visit. He found his friend alone on the veranda with someone he'd never seen before. Hasan Hammouda had just decided to turn around and leave when Safwat invited him to sit down. So he took a seat, wondering to himself when he would be able to confide his worries to his friend.

Safwat proceeded to introduce the stranger, saying, "The great Abu al-Nasr from the Palestinian resistance."

A volcano of curses erupted in Hasan Hammouda's chest. However, it wouldn't have been in good taste to leave, so he stayed put, seething all the while.

"You must have heard that we've accepted the US initiative?" Safwat asked him.

"Yes," he replied coolly.

"That's what we've been discussing."

"Pardon me," Hasan Hammouda replied indifferently, "but I'll have a drink. I'm exhausted."

As for the great Abu al-Nasr, he went on with what he had been saying before he was interrupted by Hasan Hammouda's arrival.

"However, the cause has another side to it, since it extends over time and isn't the concern of this generation alone. Furthermore, there's no reason why it shouldn't happen that, at a certain point in time and due to some necessity that's momentarily greater than we are, a decision is made to sacrifice a valiant group of Arabs for the good of the Arab nation as a whole. However, the final word will remain a sacred mystery hidden in the realm of the unknown, just as its birth will remain subject to the will. For either we die as unsung heroes whose loss no one mourns, or we live a life of dignity as we ought to."

The words came pouring out of his mouth like a tumultuous wave.

As for Hasan Hammouda, he listened to him with taut nerves, his eyes shut and his hand clutching a glass in which nothing but the dregs remained.

Glossary

Amm: Uncle. It is used in Arabic as a title of respect before an older man's name.

Anwar Wagdi: (1904–1955) a famed actor, producer, and director of Syrian origin who partnered successfully with his wife, Egyptian actress Layla Mourad. He played leading roles in and/or directed ninety-two films between 1932 and 1955.

June 5 defeat: A reference to the Six-Day War of 1967 between Israel on one side, and Egypt, Jordan, and Syria on the other. In May 1967, Gamal Abdel Nasser expelled the UN peacekeeping force from the Sinai Peninsula, where it had been stationed since the 1956 attack on Egypt by Britain, France, and Israel (the so-called Tripartite Aggression). On June 5, after Egypt had amassed 1,000 troops on its border with Israel and closed the Straits of Tiran to ships flying Israeli flags, Israel launched a preemptive strike. Jordan, which had a mutual defense treaty with Egypt, then attacked West Jerusalem and Netanya. By the end of the conflict on June 10, 1967, Israel had gained control over the Sinai Peninsula, the West Bank, the Gaza Strip, and East Jerusalem.

Sidi al-Bayyumi: A charismatic and somewhat controversial sheikh who was known for his ability to make even criminals repent, Ali ibn Hijaz al-Bayyumi (d. 1769) established a Sufi order known as al-Bayyumiya and held regular dhikr sessions at al-Zahir mosque outside al-Husayniya in Cairo.

shisha: A water pipe.

Taamiya: A mixture of mashed fava beans, parsley, and spices formed into balls and deep-fried.

"The 1919 generation": A reference to the Egyptian Revolution of 1919. Following Britain's exile of revolutionary leader Saad Zaghloul and other members of the Wafd party in 1919, Egyptians from many walks of life—from students to lawyers and postal, telegraph, tram, and railway workers—protested by engaging in acts of civil disobedience over a period of several months. This led ultimately to British recognition of limited Egyptian autonomy and the implementation of a new constitution in 1922.

The Urabi Revolution: Led by Colonel Ahmad Urabi, the Urabi Revolution was an uprising in Egypt between 1879 and 1882 against the Khedive (Ismail Pasha) and European influence in the country after a period of European occupation, corruption, misgovernment, and financial ruin.

Modern Arabic Literature
from the American University in Cairo Press

Bahaa Abdelmegid *Saint Theresa* and *Sleeping with Strangers*
Ibrahim Abdel Meguid *Birds of Amber* • *Distant Train*
No One Sleeps in Alexandria • *The Other Place*
Yahya Taher Abdullah *The Collar and the Bracelet*
The Mountain of Green Tea
Leila Abouzeid *The Last Chapter*
Hamdi Abu Golayyel *A Dog with No Tail* • *Thieves in Retirement*
Yusuf Abu Rayya *Wedding Night*
Ahmed Alaidy *Being Abbas el Abd*
Idris Ali *Dongola* • *Poor*
Radwa Ashour *Granada* • *Specters*
Ibrahim Aslan *The Heron* • *Nile Sparrows*
Alaa Al Aswany *Chicago* • *Friendly Fire* • *The Yacoubian Building*
Fadhil al-Azzawi *Cell Block Five* • *The Last of the Angels*
The Traveler and the Innkeeper
Ali Bader *Papa Sartre*
Liana Badr *The Eye of the Mirror*
Hala El Badry *A Certain Woman* • *Muntaha*
Salwa Bakr *The Golden Chariot* • *The Man from Bashmour*
The Wiles of Men
Halim Barakat *The Crane*
Hoda Barakat *Disciples of Passion* • *The Tiller of Waters*
Mourid Barghouti *I Saw Ramallah*
Mohamed Berrada *Like a Summer Never to Be Repeated*
Mohamed El-Bisatie *Clamor of the Lake* • *Drumbeat*
Houses Behind the Trees • *Hunger* • *Over the Bridge*
Mahmoud Darwish *The Butterfly's Burden*
Tarek Eltayeb *Cities without Palms*
Mansoura Ez Eldin *Maryam's Maze*
Ibrahim Farghali *The Smiles of the Saints*
Hamdy el-Gazzar *Black Magic*
Randa Ghazy *Dreaming of Palestine*
Gamal al-Ghitani *Pyramid Texts* • *The Zafarani Files* • *Zayni Barakat*
Tawfiq al-Hakim *The Essential Tawfiq al-Hakim*
Yahya Hakki *The Lamp of Umm Hashim*
Abdelilah Hamdouchi *The Final Bet*
Bensalem Himmich *The Polymath* • *The Theocrat*
Taha Hussein *The Days*
Sonallah Ibrahim *Cairo: From Edge to Edge* • *The Committee* • *Zaat*
Yusuf Idris *City of Love and Ashes* • *The Essential Yusuf Idris*
Denys Johnson-Davies *The AUC Press Book of Modern Arabic Literature* • *Homecoming*
In a Fertile Desert • *Under the Naked Sky*
Said al-Kafrawi *The Hill of Gypsies*
Sahar Khalifeh *The End of Spring*
The Image, the Icon, and the Covenant • *The Inheritance*

Edwar al-Kharrat *Rama and the Dragon* • *Stones of Bobello*
Betool Khedairi *Absent*
Mohammed Khudayyir *Basrayatha*
Ibrahim al-Koni *Anubis* • *Gold Dust* • *The Puppet* • *The Seven Veils of Seth*
Naguib Mahfouz *Adrift on the Nile* • *Akhenaten: Dweller in Truth*
Arabian Nights and Days • *Autumn Quail* • *Before the Throne* • *The Beggar*
The Beginning and the End • *Cairo Modern*
The Cairo Trilogy: Palace Walk, Palace of Desire, Sugar Street
Children of the Alley • *The Coffeehouse* • *The Day the Leader Was Killed*
The Dreams • *Dreams of Departure* • *Echoes of an Autobiography*
The Essential Naguib Mahfouz • *The Final Hour* • *The Harafish* • *Heart of the Night*
In the Time of Love • *The Journey of Ibn Fattouma* • *Karnak Café*
Khan al-Khalili • *Khufu's Wisdom* • *Life's Wisdom* • *Love in the Rain* • *Midaq Alley*
The Mirage • *Miramar* • *Mirrors* • *Morning and Evening Talk*
Naguib Mahfouz at Sidi Gaber • *Respected Sir* • *Rhadopis of Nubia*
The Search • *The Seventh Heaven* • *Thebes at War*
The Thief and the Dogs • *The Time and the Place*
Voices from the Other World • *Wedding Song*
Mohamed Makhzangi *Memories of a Meltdown*
Alia Mamdouh *The Loved Ones* • *Naphtalene*
Selim Matar *The Woman of the Flask*
Ibrahim al-Mazini *Ten Again*
Yousef Al-Mohaimeed *Munira's Bottle* • *Wolves of the Crescent Moon*
Ahlam Mosteghanemi *Chaos of the Senses* • *Memory in the Flesh*
Shakir Mustafa *Contemporary Iraqi Fiction: An Anthology*
Mohamed Mustagab *Tales from Dayrut*
Buthaina Al Nasiri *Final Night*
Ibrahim Nasrallah *Inside the Night*
Haggag Hassan Oddoul *Nights of Musk*
Mona Prince *So You May See*
Mohamed Mansi Qandil *Moon over Samarqand*
Abd al-Hakim Qasim *Rites of Assent*
Somaya Ramadan *Leaves of Narcissus*
Mekkawi Said *Cairo Swan Song*
Ghada Samman *The Night of the First Billion*
Mahdi Issa al-Saqr *East Winds, West Winds*
Rafik Schami *The Calligrapher's Secret* • *Damascus Nights*
The Dark Side of Love
Habib Selmi *The Scents of Marie-Claire*
Khairy Shalaby *The Hashish Waiter* • *The Lodging House*
The Time-Travels of the Man Who Sold Pickles and Sweets
Miral al-Tahawy *Blue Aubergine* • *Gazelle Tracks* • *The Tent*
Bahaa Taher *As Doha Said* • *Love in Exile*
Fuad al-Takarli *The Long Way Back*
Zakaria Tamer *The Hedgehog*
M.M. Tawfik *Murder in the Tower of Happiness*
Mahmoud Al-Wardani *Heads Ripe for Plucking*
Amina Zaydan *Red Wine*
Latifa al-Zayyat *The Open Door*